About the Author

Now retired, Lynda Thrift is based in the West Midlands and lives with Amble's role model. She is mother to two daughters and Nonna to her grandchildren. She enjoys playing with her grandchildren, long walks in the countryside with her dog and visiting her friends. Not always at the same time, although it has been known.

When not looking after her dog, playing with her grandchildren, or visiting her friends, Lynda enjoys travelling and exploring the world.

Waggy Tails

Lynda Thrift

Waggy Tails

Olympia Publishers
London

www.olympiapublishers.com
OLYMPIA PAPERBACK EDITION

A CIP catalogue record for this title is
available from the British Library.

ISBN: 978-1-84897-850-8

This is a work of fiction.
Names, characters, places and incidents originate from the writer's
imagination. Any resemblance to actual persons, living or dead, is
purely coincidental.

First Published in 2017

Olympia Publishers
60 Cannon Street
London
EC4N 6NP

Printed in Great Britain by CMP (uk) Limited

Dedication

For Emilia Jane

Acknowledgments

I would like to thank everyone who has played a part in bringing "Waggy Tales" from a set of anecdotal stories shared over lunch to where they are today.

In particular, the book would not have been possible without the inspiration and support of Angela and Tilda, Ruth and Karen, and Anthony and Merlin.

I would also like to thank my family for their patience in humouring me as I wrote and in providing honest critique on the outputs, and in particular, Pauline. Without their insight and sometimes forthright comments, Waggy Tales would not have happened.

A final thanks to Gary Nickolls, whose help and advice was greatly appreciated.

1. An introduction

Picture a huge, yellow ball of hair with amber eyes and a very waggy tail. Mix into that image boundless energy and good humour, and that is Amble.

Amble is a loveable, but not very bright, Golden Labrador. He is ever so friendly, but suffers from 'deaf ears', which means that that he only ever hears what he wants to hear when he wants to hear it. He thinks doing as he is told is something for soppy dogs. And he is NOT a soppy dog.

However, he will do as he is told when there is no-one else around and/or where food might be involved. Sometimes.

When he was little, Amble wanted to be a Guide Dog, and help blind people. He still remembers how proud Mummy was when he got into guide dog school.

Amble also remembers how nervous he was on his first day there, but how Adele, his clever, calm older sister, looked after him.

He tried so hard to be a guide dog. But it was just too difficult. Much to his horror, Amble realised as he went through his training, being a guide dog meant that you had to do as you were told. ALL THE TIME!

Amble was much more interested in being naughty. He particularly loved hiding from the teacher in class.

But much more than this – Amble loved food. He still does. It was – and is – his most favourite thing!

Any food.

Every type of food.

And each and every food is his favourite food.

He doesn't believe in choice. He wants it all. Now.

But as I was saying – Amble wanted to be a Guide Dog, and help blind people.

One day, when he was at Guide Dog School, Amble was walking down the street with his teacher. It all started off so well. But as you will come to see, even though things start well with Amble, they rarely stay that way!

Teacher and Amble made a distinguished couple. Amble

was leading, while his teacher was led. Just how it should be. He stopped at the kerb and waited for the cars to pass. Then he crossed the road. He waited for the bus, and then guided the teacher onto the bus. He led the way proudly off the bus and onto the High Street.

And there, he smelt the most wonderful smell. SAUSAGES!

Lovely, tasty sausages, just how he knew he liked them.

So, instead of walking along the street, like his teacher told him to, he followed his nose. His button nose told him that the sausages were close, very close. He pulled on his lead, which was very naughty. Then he guided the teacher into a doorway, and ran up to the table where he knew the sausages were. All the while pulling his teacher along with him. He must have had his deaf ears on because he didn't hear anyone telling him to stop, or wait…

As he drew in another breath of the tantalising aroma, and had begun to admire the wonderful display just in front of his nose, complete PANDEMONIUM began…

Amble didn't understand why – all he wanted was to taste those gloriously tempting, mouth-watering SAUSAGES… Surely anyone could see they were meant for him? Teacher couldn't deny him those sausages. Not after he had been so good. They were his favourite thing, after all.

But as he put his front paws on the table so he could view and sniff the delicacies some more, a huge, round, red-cheeked man dressed in a white coat, began to shake his fist, and shout in deep booming voice… Meanwhile, Teacher was standing back, watching in horror.

Amble realised that he was in BIG TROUBLE.

BIG,

BIG,

BIG TROUBLE.

That afternoon, Amble was expelled from Guide Dog School… He never went back. He didn't even get a chance to say goodbye to Mummy or Adele, his sister. And he hasn't seen them since.

Amble thinks Mummy and Adele are so ashamed of him that they NEVER WANT TO SEE HIM AGAIN EVER.

Not surprisingly, since that awful day, Amble has had a deep fear of men in white coats. And as well as being so naughty, it is because he is scared of men in white coats (and especially butchers), that Amble could never become a Guide Dog!

Which is how Amble came to live with Mrs Poser in the Big-House-On-The-Hill.

2. Friends and Neighbours

Mrs Poser looks after Amble. She plays ball with him, and lets him win.

They live together in the Big-House-On-The-Hill.

The Big-House-On-The-Hill is a lovely big house, and Amble has a nice warm bed to sleep in, which he likes a lot. It might even be his favourite thing. It certainly is at bedtime!

The Big-House-On-The-Hill also has a huge garden, with a pond. Mrs Poser lets Amble play in the garden. But Amble also loves to swim in the pond, even though it can be cold sometimes and, really, he isn't supposed to.

In fact, it's very naughty to swim in the pond because it frightens the fish that live there. And Amble gets into trouble when he shakes himself dry in the house, because he splatters mud and water all over the beautiful magnolia-coloured walls.

But he doesn't really care, because swimming in the pond is his favourite thing.

But the garden also has the hated hosepipe. Mrs Poser uses it to wash Amble when he needs it. Which is usually when he has been out on a long walk and he has come home covered in mud! And as Amble and Mrs Poser have lots of very long walks, he needs to be washed by the hated hosepipe a lot. Mrs Poser often says that she is so glad that Amble is a big yellow lump because she can easily see what needs to be washed off.

Amble can confidently say that being washed by hosepipe is NOT his favourite thing!

You should also know that if Amble can find some, he just loves rolling in fox poo – it's quite his favourite thing! He thinks it smells divine. Unfortunately, Mrs Poser doesn't! And that means that being washed by the hosepipe is only the start of what happens when they get home. After the hosepipe (which is wet and cold) comes the towelling down (which isn't so bad). But if fox poo has been involved, Mrs Poser will bring out the rose oil, and rub it into his coat. Not only is rose oil not his favourite thing, Amble is certain that rose oil is his most unfavourite thing – EVER! It makes him smell like a soppy dog. An incredibly perfumed soppy dog. He hates that.

Nevertheless, Amble loves Mrs Poser. When she isn't using the hosepipe, she is kind, and loves him back. More importantly, Mrs Poser is the source of surprise treats!

Mrs Poser and Amble have lots of adventures when they go for their long walks, and they meet lots of interesting characters. Amble loves going for walks. There is so much to smell and chase.

Now let me tell you a little more about Amble's friends.

Two cats also live with Amble and Mrs Poser in the Big-House-On-The-Hill.

Wafter is the rather snooty, fluffy cat who queens it up in the Big-House-On-The-Hill. She is a superior being who wafts around the place like she owns it. Which she believes she does. Wafter disdains Amble and his type – but tolerates him because Mrs Poser may not feed her if she does not. But this does not mean that she has to like Amble. Oh no. If she can get him into trouble, she will. Not in a spiteful way though, you understand. She is a lady, and such behaviour is clearly beneath her. That said – if he wants to be stupid, then who she to stop him? He wouldn't listen anyway

Teaser is the cheeky ginger cat who also lives at the Big-House-On-The-Hill. He is an excellent hunter. He has a flawless record of success in rodent procurement, and regularly presents Mrs Poser with his trophies. Some are even still alive. However, he would prefer the easy life, even though it is his duty to protect Mrs Poser from rodents and other pests. He enjoys snoozing, especially next to nice warm radiators.

He is more tolerant of Amble than Wafter, and will, on occasion, indulge in licking competitions with him.

However, he is less successful in the licking competitions than he is at hunting. The fact that Amble is huge compared to Teaser might be the reason for this.

But let me move on. Let me tell you about Badger.

Badger is Amble's bestest friend ever.

She is a Border Collie and is full of enthusiasm and fun.

She has boundless energy and seems to have springs rather than legs.

She is a canine high jump champion.

Badger is incredibly obedient when required to be so. However, she does hate to be on a lead, and she tries to pretend that she isn't on one. She does this by pulling as hard as she can away from whoever is holding the lead!

Badger lives with Mrs Pullalong, who is Mrs Poser's best friend, on the other side of the wild open plains. Badger loves Mrs Pullalong to bits and will do anything to please her. She comes at once when Mrs Pullalong asks, and will sit as required. Badger will even walk to heel when there are other dogs around. Amble is secretly very impressed. Amble would love to behave like Badger, but he is scared that other dogs would laugh at him if he did.

Amble and Badger love to play together. So much so that they often forget where they are. And that means that they can – and do – get into all sorts of scrapes and adventures. Badger is so quick and agile that she doesn't get into trouble. However, Amble always manages to need help to get out of it.

Let me tell you a little about when Badger was little.

She was born on a cold wet day. Her first memories are of a farm with lots of animals.

Badger didn't go to Guide Dog School like Amble. She learnt her lessons from her mother at home, and she excelled in rounding up sheep. Badger did so enjoy rounding them up – so much so that now, when she is walking with Mrs Pullalong, Mrs Poser and Amble, she tries to round them up too!

Badger doesn't really know what she has to do when she has gathered the sheep together – because just before she got to that lesson, she had to leave home. She didn't understand why – still doesn't really.

Badger does sort of remember humans talking about her, over her. She remembers going to the doctor. But Badger didn't know what was wrong with her. She wasn't sick and her teeth were perfect. However, she did learn that her back foot wasn't as strong as her front paws. And that meant that she could never become a champion sheep dog like her great grandfather. In fact, it meant that she would have to leave home and earn her living in other ways, somewhere else.

Leaving home was quite scary, but Badger's Mummy told her that she was bright and clever, and that she was ready to find a new home. That's how things work when you grow up. Badger didn't feel at all bright or clever, or very grown up for that matter. And she didn't want to leave home. So she was very frightened. Where would she go? And what could she do? Would she like it?

She was still a bit frightened when she met Mrs Pullalong, but fell in love with her as soon as she saw her. Here was someone who loved her for who she was. Mrs Pullalong was firm, but so kind and gentle – she   made Badger WANT to do as she was told.

Badger had been so scared when she was told about her bad foot, and about having to leave the farm, but Mrs Pullalong made her feel she wasn't different, and loved her just the same. And, even better, Badger was allowed to use all the lessons she had learned at home to chase the swallows. She does find it quite frustrating though because, mainly, they don't want to be chased, and fly away.

Mrs Pullalong loves Badger to bits, but wishes that Badger didn't want quite so many walks every day.

Amble has another friend in the Big-House-On-The-Hill. Mostly, she is known as 'That Baby' by the cats. She is the most beautiful, clever and brightest grandchild that Mrs Poser has ever had the privilege to be grandma to. Mrs Poser loves her to bits. But the cats do not like That Baby. Indeed, they disdain That Baby. They know that she is a menace to catdom. She chases after them, and tries to chew their tails. They aren't allowed to fight back either, which they really do not like at all. It isn't fair! In fact, though they would never tell anyone, they are quite frightened by her!

It is just as well that she doesn't live at the Big-House-On-The-Hill, because the cats would have to consider moving if she did!

Now aged three, That Baby is exactly the same age as Amble. But she is far more sensible.

That said, she has a streak of mischief which is a mile wide and she knows no fear. Amble thinks she is the brightest, most beautiful, most intelligent and wonderful baby that he had the privilege to meet. But you mustn't forget that she is the ONLY baby that Amble has EVER met.

Amble and That Baby's friendship was forged on the altar of Christmas Dinner sausages. That Baby dropped them from her high chair and Amble gobbled them up before anyone noticed. He's a helpful soul like that. He didn't want them to mess up the carpet and get her into trouble. He still has that same helpful attitude. Indeed, Amble now regularly sweeps up any leftover sticky biscuits which That Baby leaves on chairs and gooey cake which she does still scatter on the floor…

Being helpful like this is his favourite thing.

27

3. Early days

It was a lovely day. It wasn't raining and the sun was shining. Amble couldn't remember though if it was muddy or wet.

"Come on," said Mrs Poser, picking up Amble's lead. "You've eaten too much again. You need to do some exercise to work it off."

"*That's all right*," thought Amble. "*I like going on walks – they're my favourite thing. Next to food, of course, which is definitely my favourite thing. And playing ball. That's my favourite thing too. And treats. And sleeps… and eats…*"

As Amble pondered the full range of his favourite things, Mrs Poser prepared for the walk. Although lovely, it was winter, and so Mrs Poser put on her fluffy, warm fleece. Then she pulled on TWO pairs of socks – one pair pink, the other blue – and then she tucked the base of her thick corduroy trousers into her dog-walking boots. These were waterproof and lined with even more warm things. Then she put on her waterproof jacket, put on her furry hat, and pulled out her gloves. Amble wondered if she was ever going to stop getting ready. This was SO boring. He was ready now. Why wasn't she?

Eventually, after what felt like eons of time had passed, a fully thermally insulated Mrs Poser picked up the lead, pushed some dog poop bags into her pocket ("just in case") and opened the door.

Amble had almost forgotten what was going to happen, so totally ignored her.

"Come on, Amble – WALKIES! NOW!" shouted Mrs Poser.

"*Oh – okay,*" thought Amble…

Outside, he realised the wisdom of wrapping up. It was freezing. There was a very nasty cold wind. It managed to pass through his fur and hit all the goose bumps underneath.

They crossed the road and started their walk across the wild open plains…

Mrs Poser told Amble to sit, and then took off his lead, saying, "You know the rules – DON'T SHOW ME UP!"

Amble wandered off to sniff the grass and find out who else had been this way today.

"Keep your eyes open, Amble!" shouted Mrs Poser. "You might find a football in the hedges from last night's training session if you're lucky!"

"*That's a good idea!*" thought Amble, as he sniffed into the hedge at the edge of the football pitch.

But what was that he heard? Far, far away. Right at the other side of the wild open plains – across two football pitches and the cycle path.

"*That was definitely a bark. A 'Come and Play' bark. I wonder who it is?*" he thought – and decided to investigate.

Now, although Amble's usual pace is fairly staid, when he is in a hurry he can move a lot faster. And that's exactly what he did. He took off without so much as a by-your-leave or back-in-a-minute… Poor Mrs Poser was quite shocked.

"*Where has that dog gone?*" she thought, rather agitated as well as a little cross. She was worried that he might have run back across the road and been knocked down. But he wasn't on the road. So he must have gone ahead. Thank goodness. At least he was somewhere on the wild open plains and wouldn't be knocked down!

Meanwhile, at the other side of the wild open plains, Badger was in a rush. After all, she had some serious swallow chasing to do. "Come on, Mum," she barked. "Do keep up – look, there are some seagulls. I know they aren't swallows, but I can chase them just as well. Look, watch me!"

With that, she ran off, barking and running and jumping. Full of life and happy to be out and having a run.

Suddenly, she spotted this huge yellow thing hurtling towards her. "*What on earth is THAT?*" she was wondering, when she heard it say:

"Hello – who are you? I haven't seen you before. Do you live here too? What do you do? Can I play too?"

How was she to answer all those questions at once? And if she did, would the seagulls run away and hide? It's what they usually did when she was interrupted. But before she had a chance to think of any answers, the huge big yellow thing stopped in front of her and asked:

"Can I play with you? Will you be my friend?"

She looked at his big, amber eyes, and saw the dog behind them. He wasn't a threat. He wanted to play...

Mrs Pullalong caught up with them. "Who are you?" she asked of Amble. "You're a beautiful boy. Where did you come from?"

Just as Amble was wondering how to reply, the distant screeching of Mrs Poser pierced the air.

"AMBLE – WHERE ARE YOU? COME HERE, YOU NAUGHTY DOG! NOW!"

"Is that you?" asked Badger, with a twinkle in her eye.

Amble replied, "Err yes – I did rather run off without telling her where I was going. I couldn't risk missing you, you know. You have a lovely bark!"

Before Badger could think of what to do next, Amble felt his collar being held, and realised that Mrs Pullalong was holding onto him.

"You must be Amble!" she said, and then shouted, "Over here!" to Mrs Poser.

Mrs Poser didn't know whether to laugh or cry when she finally reached the tiny group. Amble had been so naughty to run away like that, but he was safe, and even seemed to have found a friend. What should she do?

Mrs Pullalong told her how Amble had bounded up to them and sat in front of Badger. Mrs Poser said "They do seem to like each other – shall we let them play for a minute? I have a ball which they can chase."

A ball! What joy! It was Amble's favourite thing!

Amble and Badger spent a very happy time chasing after the ball. Amble was very good at chasing – but Badger was so much better. And she could catch! Amble didn't mind though

– he was enjoying having a run and bark with someone other than Mrs Poser.

As the dogs ran round and round, Mrs Poser and Mrs Pullalong started to talk too.

"It's a lovely day," said Mrs Pullalong.

"Yes," said Mrs Poser. "But that wind is awfully cold!"

Suddenly, out of nowhere, two rabbits flashed past, so quickly that neither the dogs nor the ladies realised what was happening…

The dogs stopped running. Badger looked at Amble, and Amble looked at Badger.

"What… " began Amble,.

"… Was that?" finished Badger.

As they all looked on, a blur of black and white fur rushed past them, shouting "Sorry, can't stop. Chasing rabbits, you know."

Badger repeated. "WHAT was that?"

Mrs Poser asked the same question of Mrs Pullalong.

As they watched, they realised that the black and white blur was actually another Border Collie dog. As he followed the rabbits, he, in turn, was being followed, at a somewhat greater distance, by a man with a dog lead round his neck.

"Sorry about that," he shouted to the ladies. "He does like to chase the rabbits – though I don't think he would know what to do with one if he caught it!"

"Goodness!" said Mrs Pullalong. "He did quite make us jump!"

At this point, the black and white blur came rushing back.

"Hello!" he barked to the two dogs, who were now standing quite still. "Didn't see you there! Got a bit carried away. Almost had them but the little blighters ran into the bramble patch. Hate brambles… They stick to my fur and it hurts like Billy-o when I have to have them taken out."

"You don't have to tell me," sympathised Badger, nodding her head.

"Hello!" said Amble, not wanting to be left out. "I've got a ball!"

"But who are you?" muttered Badger as she sniffed this strange yet almost mirror-like image of herself. He looked so much the same, and yet, as well as being a boy, there was something quite different about him. Then she realised – he had one blue eye and one brown eye. It was quite disconcerting!

Meanwhile, the man with the dog lead introduced himself. Turns out his name was Gentleman Jim, and his companion with one blue eye and one brown eye was called Magic. "*Well,*" thought Amble, "*now that we all know who we are, can we please play with the ball some more?*"

But Mrs Poser had other ideas.

"It's very chilly here," she said, stating the obvious. "I am getting rather chilly. But I live just over there. Would you like to come home for a cup of tea?"

The other two humans needed no second invitation. The thought of sitting in a warm room with a hot drink was very appealing. Although – they asked, as they turned to accept – what about the dogs?

"Amble would be delighted to have his two new friends to play," asserted Mrs Poser. "Wouldn't you?"

"Oh, yes please!" came the reply, with a very waggy tail... "My favourite thing!"

4. Kitty Paradise Lost

Back at the Big-House-On-The-Hill, Teaser and Wafter snoozed on, oblivious to the fact that their peace and tranquillity were soon to be rudely interrupted.

It had been a long day for them both. They had been up and about well before dawn on rodent patrol. Teaser had had more success than Wafter today – he had captured two of the little pests, and deterred several more from coming into the house. It really was quite irritating the way that all the neighbourhood waifs and strays felt that they had right of entry to the Big-House-On-The-Hill just because there was an easterly wind and the temperature was minus three (again). But hey ho – that's what kept Teaser and Wafter in a job, so they had to grin and bear it.

As the two cats slept, they dreamed of how life used to be before Amble had arrived…

The Big-House-On-The-Hill was a feline haven. If you knew where to go, there were the best cosy beds on this side of the wild open plains. And the food was just fantastic. Amazing. Neither Wafter nor Teaser had eaten so well anywhere else. This place beat the best restaurants, with tasty delicacies such as lightly poached chicken in cream sauce… or even fresh mice! Oh, how the thought of food made Teaser purr with delight. Even that old fussbudget Wafter couldn't complain!

And Wafter really was a fussbudget. Indeed, thought Teaser, she really did think that she was better than anyone else in the Big-House-On-The-Hill. Even her little pink nose was snobby. She could fluff up her fur better than anyone else he knew, and had the most magnificent expression of disgust, which she used on Amble on a regular basis. Not that the stupid pooch ever noticed. He was far too focused on his favourite things. Which seemed to be just about anything.

Teaser thought back to when Amble had first arrived, and his purr disintegrated.

It was Christmas Eve. All the family had gathered at the Big-House-On-The-Hill. Mrs Poser had worked her socks off getting the place ready. There was a houseful of people – and all of them family so you couldn't be rude to any of them. Wafter had already decided that discretion was the best course of action and had taken up residence in the potting shed. Teaser wished he had the nerve to join her.

It wasn't that he disliked the family. But they all seemed besotted with That Baby. Only two years old – but Teaser knew that she was already a menace. Before she could crawl, she was able to grab him by his tail. But he couldn't scratch her to get away. Oh no – any attempt at such behaviour was definitely not on. Mrs Poser had made that very clear. So Teaser had hidden himself under the settee next to the front door – and next to the lovely warm radiator. It was a great hiding place.

He remembered a knock at the door, which jolted him awake and into instant alertness; ready for battle or –if he was to be honest – running away.

Mrs Poser went to the door and opened it. A booming voice said, "He's here if you want to see him!"

"*What? Who? How?*" thought Teaser, in quick succession.

"*This has never happened before in all my Christmas Eves here!*"

But Mrs Poser walked smartly out of the door and Teaser could tell she was excited.

When she came back, HE was with her. And HE was even more excited than Mrs Poser. He ran round everything and everyone, sniffing and licking. And even worse, he discovered Teaser, in his hiding place, poked HIS head under the settee, and gave Teaser the biggest, wettest lick Teaser had ever had.

"*Yuck!*" thought Teaser, as HE said: "Hello! I'm Amble and I think I am going to live here. Who are you? Are you friendly?"

"No!" said Teaser, and ran away to the potting shed to alarm Wafter with this latest disruption to the household. This was going to be worse than That Baby. At least she only stayed for a few days at a time. It looked like Amble could be here FOREVER!

Wafter was fast asleep on a pile of cosy old cardigans which she had commandeered when she first decided to use the potting shed as her safe house.

"Wake up!" shouted Teaser. "Wake up! This is REALLY IMPORTANT! You need to wake up NOW!"

Wafter sleepily raised her regal head and glared at Teaser.

"This had better be good," she said, unsheathing her claws one at a time. "You know that I don't like to be disturbed. AT ALL. EVER. End of story."

"I know, and I am so sorry. But it's an emergency!" puffed Teaser.

"Really?"

Wafter didn't believe that anything could be so serious that it should disturb her royal sleep. Her ancestors had guards to make sure that such things never happened. But then, in those days, cats were Gods. The Ancient Egyptians certainly knew their place and behaved appropriately. How things change. Not for the better.

"They've got a dog!" gasped Teaser. "A huge, yellow amber-eyed dog! With dog breath and licks!"

"WHAT?!" shuddered Wafter, shocked to the core. This was worse than her worst nightmare!

"Yes – and he's here to stay for ever!"

"Well, if that's the case, I am going to disappear! That will make Mrs Poser sorry!" huffed Wafter, and promptly snaked out of the cat flap.

Meanwhile, back at the Big-House-On-The-Hill, Amble was being introduced to the family. They all thought he was adorable. They loved his amber eyes. Amble was VERY excited.

"Are you going to be my forever family?" he snuffled… "and be my favourite thing?"

5. Peace is shattered at the Big-House-On-The-Hill

Teaser woke up with a start. His lovely peaceful dream had turned into a nightmare of a memory. And if he wasn't mistaken, he could hear noises crunching up the gravel drive. This wouldn't be good; he just knew it in his bones.

Teaser was right. He had heard walkers crunching their way up the drive to the Big-House-On-The-Hill.

Mrs Pullalong, Mrs Poser and Gentleman Jim were sharing stories and laughing. Amble was leading the way and showing off. Meanwhile, Badger and Magic did their best to try and round everyone up.

"This is my house," Amble stated grandly, as they all reached the gate. "It has a pond. With fish. And it's just the right size to swim in. It's my favourite thing."

That got Badger and Magic's attention straight away. Water. Just the ticket! And the little fishes to nibble your toes made it all the more enticing.

As Mrs Poser walked up the garden path and opened the front door, the dogs made a dash for the pond in the garden.

SPLASH! They all leapt in together. And then realised just how cold the water was.

"That was refreshing," said Badger.

"You're polite!" shivered Magic. "It's flipping freezing!"

"Let's go inside and see what's happening. I bet there are some treats we can have," said Amble, his mind already thinking of crunchy meat flavoured favourite things...

The dogs dashed in through the still open door. As they got inside, they shook themselves and water sprayed all over the magnolia-painted hallway. And all over Mrs Poser and Mrs

Pullalong, who just so happened to be in the way! Gentleman Jim laughed.

From his cosy spot, under the sofa by the door, Teaser looked on in horror. Not one, not two, but three of the horrible things. In his house. They hadn't spotted him yet, but they were between him and his safe place up the stairs. What to do? Should he risk being spotted and make a dash for the stairs? Or should he stay under the settee and hope they wouldn't see him. He thought back to that fateful Christmas Eve and made his decision – RUN!

He was fast. But not quite fast enough.

Amble saw him first – and shouted, "Teaser – come and meet my new friends!"

But Teaser was having none of it. He had managed to avoid any more wet licks since that Christmas Eve – and he wasn't going to hang around to have three times the number…

The three wet dogs ran after Teaser, shouting for him to wait. No chance. He took off up the stairs and into Mrs Poser's bedroom where he knew Amble wasn't allowed. Neither was he, come to think of it – which meant it must be safe, didn't it?

Mrs Poser shouted for Amble to "Come here!"

Mrs Pullalong shouted for Badger to "Come here!"

Gentleman Jim shouted for Magic to "Come here!"

And what do you think happened? That's right. Absolutely nothing.

The dogs heard the shouts, but decided to ignore them. Either that, or they all had their deaf ears on. And they wanted to meet Teaser. And lick him.

Teaser dashed under the bed. Six paws pushed up against him – but they couldn't get close. Phew! He was safe.

But it got worse! What Teaser hadn't realised was that Wafter was fast asleep on the bed. Wafter didn't stay that way for long. Not with all that noise and shouting.

Wafter leapt up in horror. The three excited and wet dogs ran after her.

Chaos erupted.

Wafter ran down the stairs. The dogs followed. She jumped through the kitchen cat flap, ran along the garden lawn and through the potting shed flap to safety.

"*Thank goodness cat flaps are for cats and only cats,*" she thought.

The dogs ran back upstairs. If they couldn't meet Wafter, they could still say hello to Teaser.

Magic showed Amble and Badger how his rabbit chasing technique might work here. It was highly successful in flushing out rabbits, so it should work to get a cat out from under a bed.

"First you have to leap at them, and make them jump," he shouted, as he bounced towards where Teaser was hidden…

Badger and Amble followed his example.

They were getting way too close for comfort, and Teaser decided that it might be wise to follow Wafter's example, and exit. Pronto!

Teaser made a run for it. He ran down the stairs.

"Over here," shouted Magic. "I told you it worked. Follow me!"

As he barked after the terrified cat, Amble and Badger needed no second invitation. They followed Magic's example, and barked and leapt to try and catch up with Teaser.

Teaser only just made the cat flap in time. "*Thank goodness he was a champion jumper,*" he thought, as he hurtled through the narrow space and into the safety of the back garden.

Meanwhile, all three dogs were barking and yapping at the door.

"Come back and say hello!" shouted Amble.

"Come here and fight like a dog!" growled Magic.

"Can I round you up?" yapped Badger. "I'm very good at it!"

But above all this noise, there were other voices. Angry and shouting…

"AMBLE! COME HERE!"

"Magic – BEHAVE YOURSELF!"

"BADGER – WHAT DO YOU THINK YOU ARE DOING?"

All three dogs realised at once that they were in big trouble. Now that Amble thought about what they had done, he remembered that Mrs Poser had told him over and over again to NEVER chase the cats. EVER! And he had.

Even worse, he had been told that he was NEVER allowed in the bedroom. Ever. And he had just run in there, with his two friends. He looked back into the bedroom, which now had a flurry of muddy paw prints on the cream carpet. Oh dear – what would happen now?

As for Badger and Magic, they realised that they had got their new friend into trouble, and that wasn't good.

They all three slunk downstairs, their tails between their legs, and worried about what would happen next…

"You naughty dogs! What were you thinking?" shouted Mrs Poser.

"I don't think they were thinking – that was the problem!" said Mrs Pullalong.

"Well, we can't have them behaving like that in the house," said Mrs Poser. "They can play outside!"

Mrs Pullalong and Gentleman Jim agreed and that was that. Amble, Badger and Magic were so relieved that this was their punishment. In fact, it didn't really feel like a punishment because the garden had so many interesting smells, and it was quite clear that a fox lived nearby, and if they were lucky they might be able to track him down and ask if he wanted to play!

As he tried to avoid being rounded up again, Amble looked into the house through the window. Mrs Poser, Mrs Pullalong and Gentleman Jim were drinking hot steaming mugs of tea, and there was a plate of lovely tempting chocolate biscuits on the table. Amble loved chocolate biscuits and would try to steal them if he got half a chance. They were his favourite thing! Which isn't good because chocolate is very bad for dogs. It makes them sick.

Amble saw that Teaser was sitting on Mrs Poser's lap, and that he was looking rather smug and very cosy and comfortable. Teaser looked up, and he saw Amble. Amble could tell that Teaser was purring with pleasure. Mrs Poser was being extra attentive to him to help him recover.

Amble looked back towards his friends, who were still dashing around the fish pond and realised why Teaser was looking so pleased. Teaser was sitting with Mrs Poser – which as we all know, is Amble's rightful place. Especially when Amble and Mrs Poser watch TV together.

More importantly, Teaser was inside in the warm and Amble wasn't! And Teaser knew this. Teaser looked very smug indeed. Now Amble knew he was being punished. Oh dear!

After what felt like forever, Mrs Pullalong shouted for Badger, and Gentleman Jim called Magic. Leads were picked up, coats put back on, and they all left. Amble sidled up to Mrs Poser. He was very sorry for all the upset he and his new friends had caused. Teaser glared at him from the other side of the room.

"You are in so much trouble, now!" said Teaser. "I wouldn't be at all surprised if they sent you back! All that chasing – of me, and Wafter, and the muddy paw prints in the bedroom. You are in so much trouble!"

Oh no, and oh dear. Amble knew he'd been naughty, but he really hadn't thought about what might happen next. He didn't want to leave here, he loved it here. He wanted it to be his forever home forever.

"Well!" said Mrs Poser. "That was an interesting walk!"

She went upstairs. Amble followed her – but not too closely, because he was frightened – he knew that they had left her bedroom in a mess. What would happen now? Would he be sent away?

Mrs Poser looked round the shambles of her room. And sighed. A long, deep, resigned sigh.

"Oh, Amble – what a mess!" she cried. "It's just as well that changing the bed sheets and cleaning this room was my next job today!"

Amble realised that Mrs Poser was sad but not angry. He'd let her down. But she wasn't going to send him away. What a relief!

Amble was so happy that he wasn't going to be sent away. He jumped up to Mrs Poser, and tried to give her the biggest lick in the world.

Mrs Poser said, "Oh, Amble – you are such a naughty dog. But I know it wasn't just you. So I won't make a fuss this time. But! If! You! Ever! Do! Anything like this again, you will be in so much trouble!"

Then, she looked at Amble, who had his head down and his tail back between his legs and was looking very sorry. She took pity on him, and said, "I shouldn't tell you this now, but you will see Badger again soon. We have arranged to have a walk again next week!"

Amble looked at Mrs Poser, and his tail wagged with joy. Not only had he been forgiven, but he would meet his new friend again. And go for a walk with her again. And chase balls with her again – all his favourite things.

6.   Christmas

Amble was in bed – his favourite place. Mrs Poser had to go out. Amble didn't know where she had gone, or how long she would be. So, he thought that he should rest until she returned, then they could go on another nice long walk – his favourite thing, you know.

As he lay there, Amble thought about how happy he was.

He had now lived at the Big-House-On-The-Hill for more than a year, and during that time he had been so very busy.

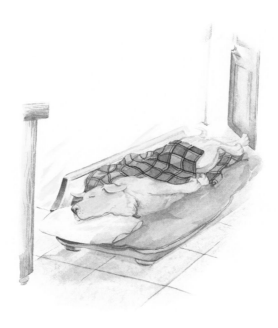

He had had to train the postman to give him the mail and the newspaper boy to let him have the paper. All that had taken quite a while. Humans aren't always easy to train, you know.

Then he had had to negotiate a peace treaty with the two cats. That took some time as well, because cats are not natural negotiators. Not unless you agree with their view and theirs only. And Amble just couldn't. He wasn't allowed out of the house without Mrs Poser, so there was no way that he would have been able to take over any of the night patrols so that cats could sleep more.

Amble had also had the task of learning about the wild open plains, and where the best smells were. It hadn't been easy because there were so many and all so different.

But now, after living with Mrs Poser for over a year, he felt that he had settled in. He enjoyed life with Mrs Poser.

As he snoozed, he dreamt of the fun he had had since coming to the Big-House-On-The-Hill. Mainly, this comprised nice quiet walks, although much, much more had happened too.

He had particularly happy memories of his second Christmas at the Big-House-On-The-Hill.

Thinking back, Amble realised that he hadn't really known what Christmas was at first. They hadn't taught him about that at Guide Dog School. Or if they did, he wasn't listening, which – to be fair – was probably far more likely. Not that it mattered – he hadn't known what Christmas was and that was that!

Amble knew that he had arrived at the Big-House-On-The-Hill one Christmas Eve – but he had been so nervous and excited then, he really couldn't remember anything about it. No, his first real memories of Christmas began the next time it came. And it was just the best!

Amble remembered how he had first sensed that something was going to happen. Mrs Poser started to become really, really stressed and bad tempered – something that she never was, except of course, when he had been naughty – and that was only right. But this was very different. Every day, she was grumpy. And he hadn't done anything wrong at all!

Then the postman started to bring lots of letters and parcels. Amble really liked letters and parcels. In fact, Amble really, really loved taking the letters from the postman and bringing them to Mrs Poser. He would run at full pace to the postman to make sure he got the letters, which made the postman jump! Amble particularly enjoyed that bit.

Then, when Amble got the letters, he would find Mrs Poser wherever she might be (and sometimes he got the impression that she didn't really want to be found!). He would then follow her around until she took the letters from him. It was his favourite thing, and such a help, Mrs Poser said.

But now the postman was bringing so many letters and parcels, Amble couldn't possibly carry them all. He simply couldn't cope. There were too many to carry at once. What was going on?

Teaser watched Amble's confusion and laughed. "Don't you know what's happening?"

"No," said Amble. "Do you?"

"Oh yes… " and Teaser began to explain.

Apparently, Christmas was coming. It was a special family time, when everyone has to be nice to each other and they give each other presents.

"And you eat, and eat, and eat… then you eat some more. Then fall asleep." said Teaser.

Amble liked the sound of that. In fact, Christmas could become his next favourite thing!

"I got Mrs Poser a big fat juicy mouse one year… " Teaser went on. "She told me that I was a great hunter and was so pleased… So the next year, I made sure that the mouse was alive. Thought that would make it an even better treat. Maybe even one of her favourite things. But for some reason, she didn't want to keep it and took it outside and let it go. After all that hard work!"

Amble wandered upstairs. He loved talking with Teaser, but his really favourite thing was to stay close to Mrs Poser. She had disappeared into the bedroom where HE WAS NOT ALLOWED. But that didn't stop Amble from poking his head round the door.

Mrs Poser was sitting in the middle of the floor. She was surrounded by mysterious boxes and sheets of brightly coloured paper. Every so often, she pulled out a roll of tape and cut it into pieces and used the pieces to fix the paper to the boxes.

Amble hadn't noticed Wafter come up behind him.

"That's called present wrapping," she huffed. "I don't know why humans do it. All that happens is that the paper is ripped off again and makes a real mess. Even worse than one you can make."

"*Oh,*" thought Amble. "*I will look forward to seeing that. Mrs Poser always says that I make the most mess. It's my favourite thing!*"

Later on that afternoon, Mrs Poser went to the front door. A man was standing there with a tree in his arms. Amble realised that this was exactly what Wafter and Teaser had said would happen next. The man brought the tree in and stood it up next to the fireplace. It all looked very odd – but not as odd as it did later on when Mrs Poser had decorated it with tinsel, glass balls and fairy lights. What was that all about?

Next – and again as Wafter and Teaser had predicted – there was another knock at the door.

Even before Mrs Poser opened it – he recognised the smell from long ago – SAUSAGES!

OH NO! That meant that there was a man in a white coat at the door – and Amble really was frightened of men in white coats.

He thought back to the incident at the butcher's which had him expelled from Guide Dog School. Amble was so scared that he barked, and barked and barked…

Mrs Poser came rushing to the door. She grabbed Amble by his collar and said, in a firm voice "No, Amble. COME HERE!" And with that, she put him in the front room and closed the door.

Amble waited and listened. He couldn't hear much at all but he did hear the front door slam, and Mrs Poser's footsteps walking past. He heard her put something down and then come to the front room door.

"I told you it's all right – the nasty butcher man has gone now. You can relax! Come and see what we will be eating for dinner tomorrow!"

Amble followed Mrs Poser into the kitchen, where on the worktop next to the sink was the most enormous turkey, already in its tray and ready to pop into the oven. Next to the turkey was a huge parcel of bacon, and an even bigger pile of sausages – just like the ones that had got him into so much trouble all those years ago!

"Don't worry, Amble – this isn't all for you!"

"*Oh!*" thought Amble. "*So much for the spirit of Christmas...*"

Mrs Poser went on. "Tomorrow, we are going to have visitors – your sisters are coming with Little Annie!"

Amble was confused. His sister was a fully qualified Guide Dog who didn't want anything more to do with him. Not since he got expelled from Guide Dog School. So what did this mean?

Wafter wafted over. She laughed when she saw Amble's confused expression.

"She means her children – and That Baby!"

Both the cats had told Amble about That Baby, and he was worried. Was she as dangerous as they said? Did she really want to pull all their tails off and chew them? Would she want to do that to him as well?

All he could do was wait until Christmas Day…

Amble remembered how nervous he had felt as that Christmas morning dawned. And it started much, much sooner than most days because Mrs Poser got up very early indeed.

"I have to start the oven so that the turkey will be ready for Christmas dinner!" she said, as she stumbled downstairs in her dressing gown.

Amble didn't really know why the turkey had to be cooked. It looked and smelt perfect just as it was. But these humans are strange creatures, and it must be important if Mrs Poser got up this early to make it happen.

The next few hours seemed to be filled with Mrs Poser rushing from the cupboards to the sink, from the sink to the fridge, from the fridge to the saucepans – and all this to make sure there was a Christmas dinner. She nearly fell over Amble a couple of times as he struggled to keep up.

The chaos was suddenly interrupted by the front door opening, and the noise of people rushing in… Amble wondered what to do. That Baby and her parents had arrived. Now he would find out the truth.

Mrs Poser rushed forward from the kitchen, kissed her daughter, said hello to her son-in-law and asked, "Well, where is she?"

"She's fast asleep in the car – we didn't want to wake her just yet so we've left her for a few minutes. It's okay, Aunty is sitting with her so you don't need to worry."

As Mrs Poser put the kettle on to make the first of copious amounts of tea which the family seemed to live on, Aunty walked in with a wriggly dark haired bundle in her arms.

"She's awake," she said.

"Oh, I can see that," said Mrs Poser, and then to the bundle,

"Come to Grandma, you delightful, beautiful darling!"

"That's odd," thought Amble. *"That's the tone of voice she uses with me. What does this mean?"*

He was soon to find out. Suddenly, all work in the kitchen stopped. Everyone went into the front room and admired the Christmas tree, which now had all the parcels he had watched being wrapped underneath.

The wriggly thing smiled at Amble and snuggled further down into Aunt's arms.

"There are more presents in the car," said Aunty.

"Can we help? You can look after Little Annie while we set the table," said Son-in-Law.

Mrs Poser needed no second invitation. She took That Baby from Aunty, and started to walk towards Amble.

"Amble – this is Little Annie. Isn't she the most beautiful, intelligent, lovely, adorable baby you have ever met?"

Amble looked at this small human. It had soft grey blue eyes, and it smiled again. Then, Little Annie reached out and gently touched Amble's ears, and laughed happily.

"She likes you, Amble," said Mrs Poser. "You have a friend!"

Amble was most surprised – this wasn't at all how Teaser and Wafter said That Baby would be. She might yet be the most beautiful intelligent, lovely, adorable baby he had ever met – but that was possibly because she was the only baby he had ever met!

Soon, it was time to eat. The table looked magnificent. There was a proper tablecloth on, and each place had more knives and forks than Amble had ever seen.

There were squares of brightly covered cloth in the middle of the cutlery.

"They're napkins – humans use them instead of whiskers," explained Wafter.

There were also long shiny tubes. "What on earth are they?" asked Amble.

"I don't know what they are called," replied Wafter. "But the humans pull them, they make a large bang. Folded silly hats fall out of them. Everyone laughs and then puts the silly hats on. I don't know why. Humans can be quite peculiar sometimes! I'm going to the potting shed. It's peaceful in there!"

With that, Wafter huffed off. Amble continued to watch the activities round the table. He agreed with Wafter. The humans did seem to be behaving quite bizarrely. But – as the humans kept saying, "It is Christmas!" and, that, supposed Amble, must explain everything.

That Baby was seated in a tall chair at the head of the table. Apparently this contraption kept her safe and meant that she could sit at the table with everyone else. Amble wished that there was something like that for him. All he could do was gaze up longingly at the table and at the people sat around it. He hoped against hope that food would come his way. After all, it was his favourite thing.

Mrs Poser staggered in from the kitchen. In her arms was the turkey – now all golden brown and smelling even better than before. Around the turkey were the baked sausages, bacon and even some stuffing balls. Amble peered closer at the table. In the middle were pots and pots and pots of vegetables – roasted potatoes, Brussels sprouts, carrots, peas – and lots more that he didn't know but just knew that he would like if he was given any!

Plates were handed out and Mrs Poser carved the turkey. Amble was amazed. She seemed to be cutting off all the meat, but there was still plenty left. Perhaps it was an everlasting turkey that they would dine on forever? What a wonderful idea! Everyone at the table had a plateful of everything – even That Baby.

Amble sat under her high chair. It was out of the way, but close to the food. A perfect spot, really.

Suddenly, a Brussels sprout landed on his head. Then a carrot. How odd.

Then, much to his surprise and delight – a whole sausage! This was just wonderful. That Baby was throwing food to him! With that, he fell in love with That Baby, and decided that

despite what Wafter and Teaser had said, she was his favourite thing!

Christmas dinner was over all too soon for Amble. That Baby really had enjoyed throwing food to him. It was apparently her favourite thing too! As a result, Amble had enjoyed turkey, bacon and a roast potato, as well as that sausage. He had even managed to taste something called Christmas pudding. It was full of fruit, so he supposed it was healthy. But he ate it anyway!

The table was cleared and everyone went into the front room. Teaser squeezed out from behind the Christmas tree. As he exited (and before That Baby spotted him), he whispered into Amble's ear, "Now its present time. Don't say I didn't warn you! You will be surrounded by paper galore, and That Baby will try to pull off your tail. Run away now!"

Oh my – Teaser was so right about the mess. Amble felt that he was being buried underneath all the wrapping paper. He could hear the chuckles from That Baby as she threw more paper on the floor and started to play with the cardboard boxes.

"Isn't that always the way?" said Son-in-law. "You spend ages searching out presents that you think she will like, and all she does is play with the boxes!"

Mrs Poser didn't care. She was having just a wonderful time. That Baby was sitting on her knee, and Amble was at her feet. She was happy. And, as we know, if Mrs Poser was happy, so was Amble!

There were lots and lots of presents. Mostly, they were for That Baby – "*She must be the luckiest baby alive,*" thought Amble! Everyone had brought her presents. But – and much to his delight – Amble had his very own Christmas stocking and it was piled full of gifts – all for him. There was a lovely tennis ball, a tugging rope, and even some treats to eat. Oh, he was a happy dog! His very own Christmas stocking – his favourite thing!

After the present opening had ended, Mrs Poser announced, "It's time for Christmas tea."

"*Goodness me!*" thought Amble. "*More food? This is just amazing. I can't believe this!*"

Teaser and Wafter sidled up to Amble as he sat under the table – which was heaving again with yet more food.

"Well," said Wafter. "What do you think of Christmas?"

"Oh," said Amble in a dream-like voice, "It's my favourite thing."

7. Mystery Woods

It seemed to take forever for walk time to arrive. Amble was in a frenzy of impatience.

"*It must be time now!*" he thought as he ran to the door for the umpteenth time. "*It has to be to be time! I want to go – NOW!*"

"Oh, Amble!" humoured Mrs Poser. "It's only 10 o'clock! We aren't going to meet Badger until this afternoon. There's a long time to wait yet. Come on. You can help me put the washing on the line."

This activity wasn't quite what Amble had in mind, and he didn't want to do it. But Mrs Poser had spoken and he knew that if he didn't do as he was told, he might not be allowed to play out at all! So he grudgingly followed Mrs Poser into the back garden, where she started to peg out the wet clothes.

"I don't know why I do this!" she said to herself. "It will only rain – and then I am back to square one. Very wet clothes!"

But Mrs Poser's analysis of the weather was completely wrong. It was going to be a lovely day if this morning's weather decided to stay. The sun was shining. There was no wind at all, and there were hardly any clouds in the sky.

"*Good weather,*" thought Amble. "*My favourite thing!*"

But, oh, how the morning dragged. Would the afternoon ever arrive so that he could meet up with Badger again? Badger really was his favourite thing. She was better than any walk, or stick, even – only possibly – a treat. But then, maybe not – food really, really was his favourite thing. He was a Labrador after all.

Amble went to his bed and had a snooze. He was having a lovely dream about the biggest bone you could imagine. And it was all his… he was just about to take the first lick when he heard Mrs Poser.

"Come on, Amble. We'll be late! I thought you wanted to see Badger again!"

It was two o'clock already! And at last! It was time for another adventure!

As usual, Mrs Poser took what seemed like forever to get ready. Amble couldn't work out why she needed to put on all those clothes – why didn't she like wet muddy feet? He thought they were actually his favourite thing.

Then they set off. Amble led Mrs Poser across the wild open plains and past the hedge where so many footballs hid. Amble and Mrs Poser finally reached the cycle path on the other side of the wild open plains. Badger and Mrs Pullalong were already there.

Badger ran towards Amble, and Amble ran towards Badger. They were so fast and so excited that they almost collided.

"I had to set off early. Badger just wouldn't stay still," said Mrs Pullalong.

"I had the same problem with Amble," agreed Mrs Poser.

"Well, let's go," said Mrs Poser. "I've always wanted to explore Mystery Woods!"

Amble and Badger looked at each other. This sounded like it was going to be a real adventure. Amble had heard a lot about Mystery Woods from Teaser and Wafter. It was where many of the mice and voles that they interrogated lived. From what Amble could remember – which wasn't a great deal to be fair as he didn't really listen to Teaser and Wafter unless he had to – the woods were dark and cold but full of really exciting smells and hiding places.

The entrance to Mystery Woods was from a quiet road. You had to know where to look for a gap in the trees. Once through the gap, you entered a hall of overhanging branches with ivy, where the bluebells also grew in spring. As you wandered in deeper, there was a rickety bridge over a slow running but deep stream.

Amble and Badger were in their element. There were so many holes and trees to explore. They ran this way and that. Then back again. It was all that Mrs Poser and Mrs Pullalong could do to keep up.

Badger raised her elegant black and white head and sniffed the air.

"I can smell something interesting – I don't know what it is as it's still very faint. But shall we find out what it is?" she asked Amble.

"Oh, yes please," came the reply. "I love exploring. It's my favourite thing."

And with that, our two intrepid adventurers set off without a care.

They ran on, and on, and on. Until suddenly, they realised that they were lost. In the middle of a tall green thicket of horrible stinging nettles. What was really scary was that the path seemed to have vanished.

"Oh!" said Badger, "I think we might be in a spot of bother here! I can't see Mrs Pullalong at all!"

"And I seem to have lost Mrs Poser!" agreed Badger. "This is NOT my favourite thing at all! What shall we do?"

At the other side of Mystery Wood, Mrs Poser and Mrs Pullalong were also getting worried. They had seen Badger and Amble romp off – but they had disappeared so quickly that the ladies didn't have a chance to follow them.

"BADGER!" shouted Mrs Pullalong. "Where are you?"

Mrs Poser suddenly noticed a small gap in the forest of nettles. It looked like the plants had been trampled down; and what was more, that they might have been trampled on by two sets of furry paws.

"Over here," she pointed to Mrs Pullalong. "I think they may have gone this way!"

So off they went, feeling very grateful that they were wearing long trousers and stout shoes. The nettles in this part of the wood seemed particularly vicious…

Amble was the first to hear the ladies' approach. "We're safe," he barked.

But he barked too soon. The ladies had found our mischievous explorers but there was now another, more important obstacle to negotiate – the way back! As well as being vicious, the nettles were tall – so tall that neither Mrs Pullalong nor Mrs Poser could see where they were going. So you can imagine what it must have been like for Badger and Amble. It was darkly green, full of creepy flying things, and not very pleasant at all.

They all tried to retrace their steps and walk on the crushed nettles. But that wasn't straightforward as Amble and Badger found it incredibly difficult to walk in single file behind the ladies. Indeed, now that they were safe (so they thought), Badger and Amble started to explore again.

After all, even though it was damp and dark, there were so many delicious and intriguing smells to follow...

It was slow progress, and several times, both Mrs Poser and Mrs Pullalong despaired of ever leaving this stinging jungle. They thought they would be stuck there for ever, which wasn't a nice thought. Mrs Poser wondered if their skeletons would even be found in future years! Mrs Pullalong was wishing that she had her phone so that she could call out the search and rescue helicopter!

But gradually, the nettles became less dense, and light started to filter through.

"I can see the path!" shouted Mrs Pullalong.

"The real path? Not the one the dogs made?"

"Yes – it's over here," she added, as they stumbled onto the track – much to the surprise of a couple of passing joggers!

Badger and Amble were so pleased to be back into safe territory. But they both knew that there were still consequences to face…

Badger knew that this adventure had frightened Mrs Pullalong – and that might mean that Badger would have to wear a lead next time. But even worse, Badger knew that she would have to have her fur combed when she got back – even she couldn't pretend that it wasn't tangled and full of burrs. She hated that. Oh dear.

Amble was also nervous – he knew that he faced the garden hosepipe. And the garden hosepipe is definitely NOT his favourite thing. But the smells had been so exciting that he had had to roll in them. He didn't understand why Mrs Poser didn't like them as much as he did. But he knew she didn't and that meant the garden hosepipe. Straightaway, before dinner, playtime or watching the TV.

But it wasn't all bad – at least Amble could tell Teaser and Wafter all about Mystery Woods when he saw them… and how they got lost and then got found.

And even better and more importantly – he was safe again with Mrs Poser – his favourite thing!

8. A Trip to the Seaside

The day was hot. The man on the TV said it was summer. Not that Amble knew what summer was.

The house was a flurry of activity. Clothes were being pulled out of cupboards and drawers. They were being laid on the bed and then folded up.

Mrs Poser had dug out a huge box-like contraption with wheels and handle. She opened it and carefully began to put the neatly folded clothes into it.

"I wonder what is going on," said Amble to the cats, as they all watched on with their tails twitching.

"It's not good," said Teaser in a doom-laden voice.

"No," agreed Wafter. "This is not good at all."

The cats began to explain. They had seen Mrs Poser do all this before. The box-like contraption was called a suitcase. The last time the cats had watched Mrs Poser putting her clothes into a suitcase, she disappeared for many, many days.

When this happened – which was long before Amble had joined them – the cats were left all alone except for a few minutes each day when someone came in to feed them. Not that the cats wanted company, but it was nice to have a choice. When Mrs Poser was around, they could pick or chose whether to be sociable.

"Oh dear," thought Amble. *"I'm not good by myself. I like being with Mrs Poser. What shall I do if she leaves me by myself for days and days? I know the cats won't look after me. They certainly won't take me on walks! Or feed me!"*

Amble was so upset that he decided to go to bed. He ran up to it, but when he got there – oh no – it had gone! It was nowhere to be seen. What on earth was happening? Was he going to be left on his own for days and days with no food and without a bed? This was almost too terrible to think about.

Meanwhile, Mrs Poser carried the suitcase outside. Then she went to get the car out. She really was going. Amble was beside himself with fear. He watched as she put the suitcase into the car, and saw that his bed was already folded up neatly in the boot. What did this mean?

Mrs Poser came back to the Big-House-On-The-Hill, and spoke to the cats.

"I am leaving you two in charge for a couple of days. Mrs Pullalong is going to make sure that you are fed. And I know you are going to enjoy the peace and quiet."

Then she looked at Amble who was now REALLY frightened.

"Amble – come with me. We are going in the car and we are to stay at the seaside. Just you and me."

Amble wasn't sure what the seaside was, but he didn't care. He wasn't going to be left at home.

Even better, he was going on a car journey – his favourite thing.

And even better still – he was going with Mrs Poser. Definitely his favourite thing.

He would work out the rest later. For now, it was more than enough that he was going on a trip with Mrs Poser in the car. He wasn't frightened any more. He was excited and happy.

Mrs Poser drove for many, many hours. Every so often, they would stop and rest for a little while. Amble was put on his lead and allowed to have a short sniff outside. Then, after a drink (tea for Mrs Poser, water for Amble) they got back into the car and drove on a little farther.

Eventually, they arrived at a big old house with many, many windows and a huge garden full of interesting tracks and paths.

"Here we are," said Mrs Poser, as she made sure Amble was on his lead. He didn't know where he was, so he didn't mind being on his lead. That way he wouldn't get lost – and neither would Mrs Poser.

Amble sniffed the air. It had a strange salty smell. All very strange, not a bit like home where the air smelt of the wild open plains, and rabbits.

Mrs Poser marched smartly up the steps and through the front door of the big house. Amble came with her because he had no choice. He was still on the lead. He didn't know where she was going, and was very glad that she seemed to.

There was a huge desk in the middle of the entrance hall. It had a large bowl of flowers on it – they smelt lovely but they were starting to make Amble's nose itch.

"Hello," said a voice from behind the desk. "You must be Mrs Poser, and… " as the voice came round from behind the desk, "… you must be Amble! We've been expecting you!" His head was patted before he got a chance to sniff the hand, but he decided that he rather liked the voice even if he hadn't been formally introduced.

Amble felt his lead being pulled and he and Mrs Poser followed the voice across the hall and along a very long corridor with doors on either side. At the door with a large '23', the voice stopped, turned to Mrs Poser and said, "This is your room. It has a small patio for Amble, and we have left you some water and a bag of biscuits for him!"

Hearing this, Amble felt his instinct to like the voice was right. Here was someone who knew what dogs liked. Biscuits were his favourite thing!

Mrs Poser set about settling in. Amble didn't understand what this meant at first, but quickly realised that it involved taking all of the neatly folded clothes out of the suitcase and putting them into cupboards – exactly the reverse of what she had done before setting off.

More importantly, however – it also meant unpacking Amble's bed. He was so pleased to see it. And it still smelt like home even though it had been in the boot of the car for the entire journey. What a relief.

After a refreshing cup of tea (and bowl of water), Mrs Poser picked up Amble's lead.

"Let's do some exploring!" she said.

Amble thought that this was an excellent idea, as a walk was his favourite thing, and he wanted to find out a bit more about where he was. And why it smelt so strange.

They walked onto the small patio outside the room, and looked out over the garden. An intriguing narrow track led away from the patio and disappeared behind a clump of trees. The salty smell was stronger here. What was behind those trees? Amble was about to find out…

They walked boldly through the trees. They were very dark and cool; the leaves made wonderful shadow pictures that Amble thought were quite his favourite thing. He was keen to keep on walking to see more when suddenly – as if by magic – there were no more trees. Or grass or anything really except pebbles and water – and that strange salty smell.

"*This is very, very strange,*" thought Amble as he felt his lead being taken off.

"Remember the rules," said Mrs Poser. "Don't show me up!"

At that, Amble bounded off. Or rather he tried to – but it was very difficult trying to run on pebbles – his paws kept sinking into them – which really put him off his stride. The water looked so inviting. It had been at least half an hour since he had had a drink, and he was so thirsty. But there was still that strange salty smell. What could it mean?

He eventually got close to the water's edge where the salty smell was really strong. Very odd. Amble also noticed that the water seemed to be moving in a very strange way. He was used to seeing the stream at the bottom of wild open plains. The water there was a brownish colour – not blue like here – and it certainly didn't have that strange salty smell. Or, come to think of it – those funny tufts of white…

Mrs Poser caught up – she was having trouble walking on the pebbles too.

"What do you think about this then?" she asked.

Amble looked again. He really didn't understand where he was or why it smelt so odd.

"This is the seaside," explained Mrs Poser. "These pebbles are called a beach. That water is the sea. And those white edges are waves!"

"*Well,*" thought Amble, "*That explains some of that! But I wonder what waves are and what they do. They can't just be there because they look pretty.*"

Mrs Poser laughed at Amble's puzzled expression. He really was most confused. He couldn't work out this place at all.

"You can go for a swim if you want," said Mrs Poser.

The water did look inviting. Much cleaner than the stream at the end of the wild open plains. And it was a nice afternoon.

"*Why not?*" thought Amble, and rushed on in.

While he splashed and paddled, he decided that he really was very thirsty. He looked at the water again. It did look good.

So he took a huge, thirst-quenching mouthful. And spat it out immediately. Now he realised where the salty smell was coming from. It was the sea water! Yuck!

What's the first thing you do when you have a nasty taste in your mouth? That's right – you try to wash it away. And that is exactly what Amble did. He took another mouthful. And it was still salty! Oh no!

Mrs Poser laughed and laughed as Amble kept trying to wash his mouth out!

After a couple of minutes, she shouted "Amble – come here!"

Amble leapt out of the water and ran to her. He wasn't at all sure about this sea stuff. It tasted vile.

Then as he got closer to Mrs Poser, he noticed that she had put his water bowl on the pebbles, and it was filled with lovely clean water. He tasted it. It was just right. In fact, it even tasted slightly chilled. It was so much better than the sea. He wouldn't be going near that again! That long drink was just his favourite thing.

Mrs Poser and Amble left the beach and continued into town. Now he was back on the lead because there were lots of cars and people around. He could easily have got lost otherwise. Amble thought Mrs Poser was quite right to make sure he was safe. After all, he didn't recognise any of this!

The shops on the sea front were very different to those from home. They all seemed to have brightly coloured things dangling outside. Some had toy windmills which made a loud whirling noise when the wind caught them; others had net bags containing coloured buckets and spades. Amble thought that was most odd. Who would want to dig in pebbles? Even he – who used to excel at digging – wouldn't do anything as silly as that!

Other shops smelt wonderful – Amble's nose told him that they sold his favourite things.

Some sold battered fish and chips. Amble recalled that he particularly enjoyed battered fish! That was his favourite thing

– but Mrs Poser would only give him little tastes as it was so bad for him – so Mrs Poser said! How could anything that tasted so good be bad for him? It didn't make sense!

There were also what seemed to be thousands of ice cream sellers. Amble decided that these were his even more favourite thing! He kept finding scoops of ice cream melting on the pavement. How anyone could leave anything so tempting behind was quite beyond him. And if it was left melting on the pavement, it would make an awful sticky mess.

So Amble, helpful soul that he is, licked it all up. After all, that's what he did when That Baby stayed, and everyone said he was so helpful. So he did the same with the ice cream. And do you know? Ice cream tastes quite delicious if it has some grit and dust added. Definitely Amble's favourite thing.

However, all of this investigating and licking took such a long time. Walking along the sea front and sniffing all the shops was time consuming, but very necessary. It also meant that Mrs Poser had to keep stopping for Amble, and she was starting to get cross.

"Oh, do come on, Amble! It's nearly dinner time!"

Amble's ears pricked up at the word 'dinner'. His favourite thing. He decided to stop sniffing and walk smartly.

It didn't take too long to get back the hotel. Or for Mrs Poser to find their room, with the big '23'" on the door.

Amble tucked into his dinner while Mrs Poser got ready. He really liked those biscuits. As he woofed his way through his food, he thought that it was rather odd that she was going to all this trouble. At home, all she did was wash her hands. But here she was putting on makeup, and even a dress. Mrs Poser NEVER wore dresses. You couldn't walk properly in a dress. And you certainly couldn't climb stiles.

Then, she put on a pair of shoes, the like of which he had never seen before. They made her several inches taller. They would be no good at all for walking across the fields!

When she was ready, Mrs Poser put Amble on the lead and took him to the car.

"*Oh good!*" he thought. "*We are going out!*"

But no. When he had settled in on the back seat, Mrs Poser opened the car window and closed the door.

"Now you stay here and be a good boy. Have a sleep. I am going to eat my dinner and I can't take you into the dining room. But I won't be long, so be a good boy!"

It didn't look like Amble had much choice, so he settled down and watched as the stars came. Mrs Poser had said that she wouldn't be long – but it felt like ages. Perhaps she had forgotten about him, and he would be left in the car all night. He didn't like be alone. And he didn't like to be away from Mrs Poser.

So he started to bark, and bark, and bark…

Mrs Poser came rushing out.

"What on earth is wrong?"

The Voice had also come out because of the noise.

"I don't think Amble wants to be by himself. Why don't I look after him while you eat your dinner? He can sit behind the big desk with me!"

Mrs Poser was a bit embarrassed at all the fuss. But she was also very hungry, and so she agreed.

Amble didn't care. He leapt out of the car, and followed the Voice, and sat down very politely next to her. Mrs Poser couldn't quite believe how well behaved Amble was all of a sudden. However, she decided, if Amble was happy, so was she. She could relax and enjoy her meal.

Amble had a lovely time sitting next to the Voice. If he lay flat on the floor he could see people's feet as they came up to the desk. He decided that Mrs Poser wasn't the only one wearing strange shoes! Lots of people seemed to have them on.

Mrs Poser came back too quickly. Amble was enjoying himself and didn't want to go to bed. He was having a lovely time. The Voice stroked his head all the time and told him he was a good boy. He liked that!

But he knew better than to argue, so he followed Mrs Poser back to the room with '23' on the door, and settled down for a good night's sleep after such a busy day.

Apart from that horrid salty sea, Amble could get the hang of the seaside if he tried.

Indeed, when you counted in the ice cream, he thought it really was his favourite thing.

9. What is this thing called cricket?

Amble and Mrs Poser were sitting in their favourite place at the top of the wild open plains. It was a gloriously warm sunny day, and they were enjoying a picnic.

Mrs Poser was eating a cheddar cheese sandwich, and Amble was drooling. He just loved cheddar cheese sandwiches

– they were his favourite thing. He couldn't understand why Mrs Poser hadn't made him any or, for that matter, why she wasn't sharing hers with him. He had tried everything. He had rolled over on his tummy. That didn't work. He had looked imploringly into Mrs Poser's eyes. And that hadn't worked either.

"Amble," said Mrs Poser, between mouthfuls. "You were told when you ate all your breakfast this morning that you couldn't have anything else to eat until dinner time! You can only have two meals a day, otherwise you would be the size of a house!"

Amble thought about that for a little while. He decided that if it meant he could have a cheddar cheese sandwich, he wouldn't mind being the size of a house!

Those sandwiches smelt so good. So cheesy and buttery. With fresh bread and the merest hint of mustard. Just how he liked them. Oh, how he wanted one.

Mrs Poser gave in. She just couldn't resist those amber eyes any longer.

"All right, Amble," she said, as she passed a half-eaten corner of her sandwich to him. "I suppose you deserve this!"

As Amble gulped the morsel down, it barely touched the sides of his mouth – but he thought he could taste it. Maybe he should have another bite just to make sure?

But, with horror, as he raised his eyes again, in that soulful way, which had just proved so successful, he saw that Mrs Poser had packed everything away. Even his water bowl.

"Come on then, Amble," she said. "We need to walk off all that food now."

"Harrumph!" muttered Amble. "There was scarcely a bite, never mind a mouthful!"

But he had no choice. Mrs Poser was walking on ahead and he didn't want to lose her.

As they walked alongside the hedgerows at the side of the wild open plains, Amble heard some very strange noises far away in the distance.

There were cries which sounded like "howzat", and clapping. Very odd. Then, after a pause, more noises which sounded awfully like wood hitting wood.

"Oh dear," said Mrs Poser, getting out his lead. "I hadn't realised they were playing. I had better put you on the lead till we get past them!"

Amble wasn't too happy about having to wear his lead. Not here. Not at this part of his walk. He didn't usually have to wear it here, so what was different about today?

When he emerged from beside the hedge, he saw exactly what was different about today!

Usually, the wild open plains were empty, with only Amble and Mrs Poser walking. They only rarely met others, like Badger.

Today, though, there were many, many people, all the way across the wild open plain. Some were seated by the old shed, others were standing up. Lots of them were wearing white trousers and jumpers. Amble felt a tickle of fear as he remembered men in white coats. But it was only a tickle. He decided that he wasn't frightened of these men in white trousers and jumpers because they weren't wearing white coats. But what was going on?

He saw that several men in white trousers were standing in a circle. In the middle was a long rectangle of what seemed to be bare earth. And at each end, there were three sticks in the ground, and a man with a stick guarding them. As he watched, he saw a third man run up towards one end of the rectangle, and throw a ball – a lovely, mouth-sized red ball. Amble wanted that ball. He so wanted that ball. That ball was his favourite thing. He pulled and yanked at his lead, and almost pulled Mrs Poser over several times. Why couldn't he have that ball? The man in white trousers didn't want it – he had just thrown it away. And the man with the stick didn't want it, because he had hit it away.

But hold on…

One of the men in white trousers at the side suddenly made a grab for the ball and stopped it in its tracks. Then he picked it up and threw it to another man in white trousers. Drat! That was Amble's ball. He just knew it!

"Come on, Amble," said Mrs Poser in a stern voice. She wasn't very convincing, as she was having huge problems stopping Amble from dashing up to the rectangle and snatching the ball away.

"This is why you are on the lead," she growled to Amble as she dragged him back. "I knew this would happen!"

Soon, however, they were past the strange scene and tempting red ball. Mrs Poser took off Amble's lead.

"Now we are past the cricket game, I am trusting you to be good!" she said. "But you know the rules. Don't show me up!"

Amble was never one for looking back, so he marched on across another part of the wild open plains, while Mrs Poser explained to him that he had just seen his very first game of cricket. Apparently, the wild open plains had become what was called a cricket pitch. The men in white trousers were playing cricket. They were cricketers. Whatever that meant.

The men with sticks who were guarding the standing sticks were batsmen.

The man who threw the ball away was the bowler.

All the others were apparently fielders.

All in all, it was all very strange. And, if Amble understood correctly, just a little bit boring. But there were some good bits – like throwing the ball. That was good, he conceded.

As Mrs Poser started to explain the rules in more detail though, Amble got very bored indeed. He stopped listening and started to sniff the grass.

Eventually, they got back to the garden gate at the Big-House-On-The-Hill. Mrs Poser was very tired. Amble was still sniffing the grass just a little way off when, suddenly, he caught a whiff of something VERY interesting.

Mrs Poser wearily opened the gate. Then she looked round for Amble, expecting him to rush past her and head towards the front door. It was his dinner time after all. But he was nowhere to be seen. Amble had vanished into thin air. There was not even a hint of his tail showing above the long grass over by the road. Where had he gone?

Mrs Poser ran over to the road. She hadn't heard any bangs or crashes or squeals of brakes. But she was worried nevertheless. She looked up the road and down the road. No sign of Amble whatsoever. Oh, where had that naughty dog gone?

Mrs Poser shouted his name. The more worried and frightened she became, the louder and more shrill her shouts became. And as she was very worried indeed, you had to say that she really was quite shrill indeed. But still no Amble.

Oh dear. Mrs Poser started to ask the joggers and the walkers on the cycle path if they had seen Amble. But no-one had.

There was only one thing to do. She had to retrace the walk that they had taken so long to complete and see if Amble had decided to go back.

She walked to where they had enjoyed their picnic and shouted again. And waited. Nothing happened.

Then she walked down past the hedge row, and shouted again. Nothing.

She spotted some cricketers walking up from the game. She asked them if they had seen Amble – but they hadn't.

So Mrs Poser kept walking and asking. When she had just about given up all hope, one of the walkers passing by replied, "Do you mean a big yellow dog?"

"Oh yes!" said Mrs Poser. "Have you seen him?"

"We've seen a dog that sounds like it might be him. He ran that way. He was in a terrible hurry!"

"That's strange!" thought Mrs Poser as she headed in the direction the walkers had said. *"Amble should be tired out and ready for his dinner. He should be keen to get home, not rush around on the wild open plains!"*

As she ran, Mrs Poser kept asking. And, yes, came the reply – he had been seen. She was heading in the right direction.

Mrs Poser emerged from the hedgerow, and ran towards the cricket shed where people were sitting. No-one playing cricket now. It was clearly teatime. All the players were also by the shed, drinking cups of tea from a huge urn which had been put on one of the tables. Some of them were eating sandwiches.

"Have you seen my dog?" she asked them. "He's a big yellow Labrador who loves red balls. He hasn't taken yours, has he?"

"Do you mean that dog?" asked one of the cricketers, his mouth full of sandwich.

Mrs Poser turned her head to look where he was pointing.

And there was Amble. The naughty dog. And do you know? He was surrounded by at least six of the players from the field and he had a huge smile on his face.

Amble looked up and spotted Mrs Poser. He wagged his tail but didn't move. And he kept on smiling.

As Mrs Poser got closer, she realised just why Amble was smiling.

The six players weren't just standing around Amble. They were feeding him cheddar cheese sandwiches. And he was loving it.

One of the players asked, "Is this your dog?"

"Yes," said a relieved Mrs Poser, not knowing whether to laugh or cry. "What are you doing, you naughty dog?" although it was painfully obvious. He was eating cheddar cheese sandwiches and having a thoroughly good time.

As he woofed another cheddar cheese sandwich, Amble looked at Mrs Poser and said, "I like cricket. It's not a boring game after all! It's got cheddar cheese sandwiches. And do you know? They're my favourite thing!"

10. An unexpected reunion

Summer had come to an end. And now it was getting cold again on the wild open plains.

More importantly for Amble, it was that time of day again.

Mrs Poser had thermally insulated herself and picked up Amble's lead. Amble was bouncing alongside her, excited at the thought of going for a walk – his favourite thing.

They walked along their usual path, across the wild open plains. Amble was having a lovely time, sniffing all the different smells. While he hadn't yet found a source of fox poo suitable for rolling in, there were intriguing hints and promises of possible alternatives.

Amble sniffed on. There were all sorts of smells to enjoy. There was the lovely, earthy smell from the ground, and the long grass smelt almost like fresh hay. He could track where the mice had run away from Teaser and Wafter, and he could even smell traces of the cats too. He wandered deeper and deeper into the long grass at the edges of the wide open plains, and started to sniff his way to the hedge. Smelling really was his favourite thing, you know.

Suddenly, Amble broke off from his thoughts and nasal musings to realise that Mrs Poser had disappeared. She was simply nowhere to be seen. He stopped, and listened. He could usually hear where she was if he tried hard enough. But he couldn't hear her at all. It was suddenly most awfully, scarily quiet.

Amble nervously edged his way out of the long grass to see if he could find Mrs Poser. This wasn't how things were meant to be. Mrs Poser should come looking for him. He got lost. She found him.

Amble reached the edge of the long grass, and stood to attention. He held his head high, sniffed the air and looked all around.

There she was – but such a long way away. Mrs Poser was right over the other side of the wild open plains! Amble was quite put out – how dare she run so far ahead without him. It simply wasn't on! What if she had got lost? She would be sorry then! Then, he suddenly remembered that he had done exactly that more than once himself – like when he met Badger for the first time. Now he started to understand why Mrs Poser had been so cross with him.

Amble ran to join Mrs Poser, who didn't seem to have noticed that he wasn't by her side. As he huffed his way across towards her, he realised that there was someone else with her. It was a tall man, but from where Amble was standing, he couldn't tell any more than that.

Suddenly, there was a piercing noise which made his ears hurt. He closed his eyes and opened them again. That was painful. It really hurt.

"*What on earth was that?*" thought Amble. "*I had better run to Mrs Poser and save her!*"

As he sped up his galumphing across the wild open plain, Amble was able to see the man more clearly. The man was wearing what seemed to be a necklace with a long pencil-like metal shape at the end. Amble stopped to watch. The man put the long pencil-like metal shape into his mouth and blew on it. And there it was again. That awful noise that made his ears hurt! He closed his eyes again.

"*Gosh,*" he thought. "*That must be a whistle! Now I think about it, I remember Guide Dog School used them to get my attention. And I also remember why they worked – that noise is so sharp!*"

As the piercing noise stopped, Amble opened his eyes and realised that he was no longer the only dog on the wild open plains. There was another honey-coloured creature running from the stream towards the man. And it looked ever so slightly familiar.

"*Gosh,*" thought Amble, as he ran towards the group, "*It might even be a Labrador like me!*"

The closer Amble got, the more like him the shape became.

"Hello!" he shouted. "Who are you?"

"Oh, Amble," came the reply. "Don't you remember me?"

Amble was confused. The only other Labradors that he had even known were his mother and his sister. And he hadn't seen them since he was expelled from Guide Dog School. He thought they were so ashamed of him that they 'NEVER WANTED TO SEE HIM AGAIN!'

He became very sad as he remembered that he wasn't even allowed to say goodbye to his mother before he left Guide Dog School. But all that was such a long time ago.

The other Labrador came closer to Amble and gently nuzzled his face.

"It's me," she said. "Please say you remember me!"

Amble looked into a pair of beautiful soft amber eyes, not that different to his own. Then he smelt her. He knew that smell. It had been a long, long time since he had smelt that smell, but he remembered it. And he recognised her. Even though he hadn't seen her for such a long, long time.

It was his big sister Adele. She had grown up so much. But why was she here now? Was it real?

"Adele!" he woofed joyfully. "It really is you? I'm not dreaming, am I?"

"No, Amble. It's definitely me."

The two dogs sniffed and licked each other joyfully.

Mrs Poser and the Man-With-A-Whistle had no idea what was going on. Clearly neither of them spoke Dog. But they were pleased that Amble and Adele were playing together so nicely.

"Well," said Mrs Poser, "Amble seems to like Adele!"

"And Adele likes him!" replied the Man-With-A-Whistle.

As the two dogs continued to fuss over each other, the Man-With-A-Whistle introduced himself. He was called Mr Helpful. He explained that he helped to train Guide Dogs. It's a lot more complicated that you can ever imagine.

Mrs Poser then told Mr Helpful all about Amble's rather checkered background. Much to Amble's embarrassment, it included the information that he had been expelled from Guide Dog School and that he hated men in white coats.

"Oh dear!" said Mr Helpful. "But I am sure that he wouldn't have enjoyed being a Guide Dog. Not everyone does! Every dog is different, just like humans!"

As Mrs Poser and Mr Helpful walked on a little farther, Mr Helpful explained that he and Adele had recently moved to this side of the wild open plains. He used to live far, far away in another town. Adele had joined him when she had finished Guide Dog School.

But neither Mr Helpful nor Mrs Poser realised that Amble and Adele were brother and sister. Not yet, and they wouldn't find that out for a long, long time…

That's a story for another time.

For now, they were just pleased that Amble and Adele were proving to be good friends.

Amble was quite overcome. He had missed his sister so much and had been so upset when he thought that she was ashamed of him and never wanted to see him again.

But now, Amble had found his big sister Adele. And she was so pleased to see him. Amble just jumped for joy. He was so happy now. Even though the thought of that dreadful day when he left Guide Dog School still made his tummy flip. This was definitely his favourite thing!

Adele told him that Mummy was upset at what had happened. But, in the end, she and Adele found it all rather funny. It was just awful that they hadn't seen Amble since that dreadful day. They really missed him, and were so sad when he disappeared. They never got a chance to tell him how much they loved him because he left Guide Dog School so suddenly.

"Do you remember when we were puppies, how everything was your favourite thing?" asked Adele as they wove around each other.

Amble replied, "It still is! I haven't changed. You are my favourite thing!"

Then they both laughed.

They didn't want to waste a precious second of being close, but Amble and Adele also wanted to run and play together like they used to when they were little. Which meant that they were all a bit of a tangle. Mrs Poser couldn't quite see where one dog started and the other one ended!

"But now you are a grown up! You finished your training and became a Guide Dog. Mummy must be so proud of you," said Amble.

"I'm still the same Adele whose ear you used to nibble and bite when we were babies. Do you remember?"

Amble smiled at the memory. As a puppy, nibbling and biting Adele's ear had been his favourite thing!

Mrs Poser and Mr Helpful watched the two dogs. They were having such a lovely time.

"I know!" said Mrs Poser. "I live just over there in the Big-House-On-The-Hill. Would you like to bring Adele over for a cup of tea?"

Mr Helpful thought that this was an excellent idea. After all, blowing whistles can be quite tiring.

As they walked back, Mr Helpful explained that Adele wasn't a quite a Guide Dog. She did pass all her tests, and was fully qualified. In fact – but Adele didn't know – she had been top of her class! She could have been a Guide Dog. But the teachers were so impressed with how calm and clever she was that they asked her to do a very different job to help blind people. She was going to have puppies that would, one day, become Guide Dogs too. It was a very important thing to do because there are more blind people than Guide Dogs.

Mrs Poser opened the garden gate, and Amble ran on ahead to show Adele the pond. And the fish. He was very proud of his pond. It was his favourite thing.

"Well, I would never have believed it!" said Adele "You have such a big garden, and such a lovely pond! You are a lucky dog! I can't wait to tell all my friends all about you when I next go to my Agility Class with them!"

"What's Agility?" asked Amble.

Adele explained, "It's where you run and jump over obstacles and play, and meet up with other Guide Dogs. But it is only for Guide Dogs. No-one else is allowed to join! If they did, there would be too many of us and we wouldn't get as many turns on the equipment!"

Now, as you will have worked out – Amble is not very agile, so he wasn't too worried about not going to Agility Classes. They actually sounded far too active for him. He much preferred mooching around the wild open plains.

For now, though, Amble had his favourite sister with him here.

It was just lovely. There was so much to share and catch up with. But before he could even think about where to begin, Adele suddenly became all serious.

"There is something else that I need to tell you," said Adele as they ran round the pond again.

"What's that?" replied Amble.

"I may not be able to see you again for a while."

"But we've only just found each other? That can't be true."

Amble's good mood dissolved instantly. He thought he might cry!

"Why not?" he asked sadly.

"I'm not a Guide Dog!" she stated.

"What?" exclaimed Amble. "But you finished your training. You told me so! And you go to Agility Classes. How can you not be a Guide Dog?"

Adele explained to Amble what Mr Helpful had told Mrs Poser.

"You remember that you were always the naughty one in Guide Dog School?

"Yes, "replied Amble. "And?"

"I was the calm and clever one."

Amble agreed.

"Well," continued Adele, "Because I am so calm and clever, my teachers asked if I would do something else, which would actually mean I could help more people."

Amble wondered what this could mean. It was all quite mysterious.

"I'm going to have puppies. And when they are old enough, they will be Guide Dogs too!" announced Adele.

Amble was absolutely stunned. Adele was pregnant. He was going to be an uncle. Gosh! That really was amazing. And his nephews and nieces would become Guide Dogs if they were clever enough. (And not naughty like he was).

"You're really going to have babies?" gasped Amble in delight and pride.

"Yes. My puppies will be born in a few weeks' time!" Adele told Amble. "But that means that I have to stop running around so much soon until they are here. And then all my time will be spent looking after them until they are ready to go to Guide Dog School."

Mr Helpful and Mrs Poser were also talking about the puppies. They both agreed that it would be nice if Amble could visit the pups when they were old enough. And then, when the puppies started Guide Dog School, Amble and Adele could play out again.

All too soon. Adele and Mr Helpful had to leave. Mr Helpful put on his coat and necklace with the whistle on it. Adele wore her lead.

Amble insisted on walking next to Adele all the way to the gate, and he would have followed her beyond if he could have. But Mrs Poser kept a tight grip on his collar. Amble thought he might cry again. It was so hard to say goodbye!

"You can't go with them today, Amble!" she said.

"But," she went on, "I promise that we will see Adele and her babies when we are allowed to. And you will play out with Adele again too! But not just yet."

Amble wasn't really listening. It had been a very odd day.

He had found his sister. Then she was gone again. But she was going to have puppies, and that meant that he was going to be an uncle!

And, just as importantly, although he would have to wait – he would see Adele again – most definitely his favourite thing.

11. A quick dip

By now, it was autumn, and all the trees were starting to lose their leaves. All the long grass was starting to die. So there were fewer and fewer places for the dogs to hide on their long walks. So Mrs Poser and Mrs Pullalong thought it might be a good idea to try and find some different places to walk.

Mrs Pullalong had a new book with lots of exciting ideas for walks. She showed it to Mrs Poser and they agreed to use it to help them explore further afield.

Using their new book of maps to help them, the ladies decided to take the dogs along a new path. According to the book, on the far side of the woods and far away from the cycle path, was another stream.

"Let's see what this stream is like!" suggested Mrs Poser.

But what the map didn't say, and so the ladies couldn't possibly know, was that this stream wasn't as nice as the one by the wild open plains. This one was very deep and had incredibly steep banks. Even though it was autumn, it was still lined with vicious stinging nettles which made those in Mystery Woods and around the wild open fields seem tame. Wild open plains nettles really hurt. Mrs Poser knows this because one day Amble had lost his ball in them, and she had to get it.

Even though it was now September, it was one of those really hot autumnal days. A very hot day. Mrs Poser had her sunhat on, and Mrs Pullalong wished that she had hers.

The temperature didn't stop Amble and Badger from chasing each other, and hiding behind the trees. They were having such fun.

"I wonder what they talk about," mused Amble as they raced around another oak tree.

"I can't possibly know – they do seem to enjoy chatting to each other though, which is good because they aren't watching us all the time. I like that."

"Me too," said Amble. "It's my favourite thing!"

The dogs ran and ran and ran.

Badger said, "I'm thirsty. All this exercise has made me really hot."

"Me too," said Amble, as he realised that yes, he was rather warm. In fact, the two dogs were panting!

Now, you may remember that in Mystery Woods, our two doggie friends had followed a fox track – and got very lost. You would think that they might have learnt from this adventure that following fox tracks was perhaps not a sensible thing to do.

But they were thirsty. And they just knew, as you do, when you are thirsty, that the fox track in front of them led straight to lovely, cool, refreshing water. At the bottom of the stream with steep sides and vicious stinging nettles. When you are thirsty, you don't notice details like that. Or at least Badger and Amble didn't!

"Come on," shouted Badger, as she bounced through the nettles. "The water is just down here. I can hear it."

There was a splash, and Amble heard Badger shout, "This is wonderful!" which was followed by the sound of Badger lapping up the cool water.

Well, Amble needed no second invitation – he leapt in. Another loud splash – which the ladies heard.

As Mrs Poser and Mrs Pullalong ran to see what was happening, Amble swam into the deeper water, and had a lovely long drink too.

Amble looked up the stream – it was a lovely cool scene, with overhanging branches and lots of midges flying. He looked down the stream – still the steep banks, still the nettles and still the lovely overhanging branches with reddish leaves and flying midges. It was all very peaceful really. And very pretty.

"Right," said Badger "Time for some more swallow chasing," and sprang out of the stream as if she was on springs. She ran back along the fox track and up to Mrs Pullalong.

"Hello – I don't need to guess where you have been," said Mrs Pullalong as Badger shook herself dry. "But where is Amble?"

Oh no – Badger looked back, and she could just about see a honey-coloured outline at the bottom of the steep bank lined with nettles, and still in the water.

"Come on, Amble," barked Badger. "There are swallows that want to be chased. Hurry up!"

And Amble tried. Oh how he tried. But he just couldn't climb up the steep banks. He certainly couldn't jump up like Badger had. He just wasn't that fit or agile. What was he to do? Was he going to be stuck in the stream for ever? While he wouldn't be thirsty, his paws were starting to get a little chilled. Would he be stuck in there till winter? Or even forever? What a terrifying thought! Amble really wanted to get out!

Meanwhile, the ladies stood on the other side of the nettles and wondered what on earth they should do. There was no other way down to the water – or back up from it that they could see. No, the only option was for Mrs Poser to climb down herself to try and rescue Amble.

But how on earth was she going to do that? Neither of the ladies were dressed for scrambling down a steep stream bank which was covered in nettles. Indeed, Mrs Poser didn't even have a coat or jumper with her. They looked at the nettles in horror, as Amble realised his dilemma and started to whimper.

"Oh dear – hang on, Amble. We'll work something out!" shouted Mrs Poser, which reassured him a little.

Then Mrs Pullalong looked up the stream and Mrs Poser looked down the stream. Apart from the fox track, there were no gaps. At all. There was only one choice. Mrs Poser had to get down there. When Mrs Poser reached the edge of the bank, she sat down and took off her trainers, and threw them over the nettles to Mrs Pullalong and Badger who were waiting there. After all, she didn't want to wear them in the stream and then have to walk home in wet shoes.

Then, she rolled up her track suit bottoms (so comfortable for walking in), and started to advance. Oh, those nettles were painful. Even though the dogs had trampled them down a little, there were still many stems at just the right height to hit her uncovered arms and legs.

Then she slid down the steep bank to where Amble was waiting. He did look hopeless and as she surveyed the stream, she could see why. She looked up the stream, then down the stream. She realised that there was no easy way back up without having to confront more nettles.

Oh well. First things first.

Mrs Poser grabbed Amble by his collar and turned him round so he faced up the bank. Then she pushed him from behind as hard as she could back up the bank. Amble scrambled up to safety, and to Badger and Mrs Pullalong.

Now it was her turn. Surely she could scramble back up too? But there was no one to push her.

"What are you doing?" called Mrs Pullalong, because she couldn't see over or through the nettles.

"I'm not sure," came the reply, as Mrs Poser realised that she would have to crawl over all the nettles that she had trampled down as she had got into the water. Even worse, some of them seemed to have elastic stems and were righting themselves. Getting out of the water here would be very painful indeed.

Mrs Poser thought for a moment.

"I think I will wade a bit further upstream as there may be an easier way out, and, if I am lucky, perhaps fewer nettles!" she shouted.

"Good idea," agreed Mrs Pullalong. "I will follow you from this side and when we find a place that hasn't quite as many of those horrid weeds."

Mrs Poser waded upstream. All the while, the banks were too steep to walk up, and covered in nettles.

Eventually, Mrs Poser came across an old plank which was wedged across the stream. It had come to rest about halfway up the bank. Again, she looked up the stream and down the stream, and figured that this was going to be her best and – as far as she could tell – her only option. Although the stream was becoming more shallow, it was also starting to become clogged up with rubbish – not good for bare feet. And the halfway plank would mean that she would only have to get through half as many nettles because the plank was there, halfway up the steep bank. Nevertheless, it was not an easy way through – and none of the nettles here had been trampled down at all.

What a dilemma!

Should she go up here or go back to where she had started from?

Then Mrs Poser had an idea. It wasn't elegant, and it certainly wasn't the sort of thing she would do in town, and she certainly wouldn't have even considered it if it hadn't been absolutely essential.

Mrs Poser took off her tee shirt. Then, as she stood there, wearing only her bra and rolled up tracksuit bottoms, she spread the tee shirt over some of the nettles.

Thankfully, Mrs Pullalong couldn't see a thing from where she was standing.

"What are you doing?" shouted Mrs Pullalong from behind the curtain of nettles.

"I'm taking my tee shirt off!" replied Mrs Poser.

"What?" asked an ever-so-slightly shocked Mrs Pullalong, totally confused by this turn of events.

Surely Mrs Poser wanted to escape the nettles – how was taking her tee shirt off going to help?

Mrs Poser went on to explain. "There are still too many nettles to get through, especially in bare feet. I am going to use my tee shirt to cover the nettles in front of me so I can get to the top of the bank without getting too many stings."

It now started to make sense. Not a lot of sense, it has to said, but some sense at least.

But even doing this, Mrs Poser couldn't quite reach the top of the bank. She scrambled as far as she could, then sat down on her tee shirt and shouted over to Mrs Pullalong.

"Can you throw me my shoes? But please be careful – I wouldn't want them to go in the water after we've been to all this trouble to keep them dry"

First one shoe, then the next, came flying over the nettles and landed flop, just next to Mrs Poser – Mrs Pullalong really was quite a good shot! Mrs Poser put her shoes back on. Her feet squeaked in them now as they were still wet. But it was better than having to walk all the way back in wet shoes. And she was still stuck in the middle of a vicious nettle bed.

Then Mrs Pullalong had a cracking idea which could solve Mrs Poser's remaining problem of getting through the rest of the vegetation.

"Put your tee shirt back on, Mrs Poser," shouted Mrs Pullalong. "And then I will be able to help!"

Mrs Poser did so – but had to wear it inside out because it had collected lots and lots of burrs as it lay on the nettle bed. It did look odd – with a huge red label saying it had been in the sale still on it!

When she had her tee shirt back on and was respectable again (or as respectable as you can be with an inside-out tee shirt covered in burrs and a big red label), Mrs Pullalong shouted again.

"Are you decent? Good! I'm going to throw you one end of Amble's lead. I will hold the other end and I will pull you up the last bit! You'll still have to go through those nettles, but we can make it quick"

Well, what a good idea. Although Mrs Poser was going to be stung, this would mean it wouldn't be as bad.

Meanwhile, Amble and Badger watched – half afraid at all this madness, and half amused by the thought of Mrs Poser with her tee shirt on inside out!

Suddenly, Mrs Pullalong took the strain, and almost fell over backwards into Amble and Badger. Indeed, she would have if they hadn't jumped out of the way, just in time.

As she stumbled, Mrs Poser was dragged into view, looking quite dishevelled but so happy to be on dry land with no nettles again.

"Thank you ever so much! That was such a clever idea. And without your help in heaving me up, I don't know what I would have done!" said a very grateful and relieved to be back where it was safe Mrs Poser.

But she was still very, very stung. Goodness me – the nettle stings did so tingle and itch.

Mrs Pullalong found some dock leaves – which are nature's way to stop the itching – but Mrs Poser had so many stings there really weren't enough of them to really have any sort of impact. They were all the way up her arms and all the way up her legs to where the track suit bottoms had been rolled up. They were all going quite red.

Amble and Badger were very subdued. Amble realised how close to ABSOLUTE DISASTER he had been. If Mrs Poser hadn't have come after him to rescue him, he would still be in the stream, and would never have got out! And, if Mrs Pullalong hadn't been there, Mrs Poser would still be in the stream instead.

Badger was just so proud that Mrs Pullalong had been able to rescue Mrs Poser! It was such a clever idea to use Amble's lead! She would never have thought of it!

"That was more than we bargained for when we set off," said Mrs Poser, as she scratched her arms. "Please don't ever do anything like that again, Amble!" knowing full well that he probably would.

Mrs Pullalong became very practical when she saw how many nettle stings Mrs Poser still had.

"Let's get you home."

The sorry group made very slow progress, because Mrs Poser's shoes were starting to rub as well as squeak. Mrs Poser was so worried that she would get painful blisters on her feet. They are not a good thing to have when you have to take

Amble for long walks. Sore feet and legs and arms were making Mrs Poser quite grumpy!

But after what felt like an age, they arrived back at the Big-House-On-The-Hill.

"Let's put some camomile lotion on those stings and I can make you a cup of tea," volunteered Mrs Pullalong.

That sounded like a very good idea to Amble, who was starting to cheer up. Mrs Poser, however, decided that she must have a shower before doing anything else. Then she could put the soothing lotion on her stings.

When she had had her shower, and changed her clothes, Mrs Poser settled into her favourite chair. As she nibbled on a ginger biscuit and sipped her tea, she started to feel a little better. Although those nettle stings really did sting, the camomile lotion helped.

"That wasn't quite the walk we had planned, was it?" stated Mrs Pullalong.

"At least it was memorable," replied Mrs Poser. "And it could have a whole lot worse! At least I had sensible shoes and trousers on. I don't have too many stings on my legs!"

On that note, Mrs Pullalong and Badger decided to leave and let the bedraggled pair recover from their adventure.

As they watched Mrs Pullalong and Badger disappear back out to the wild open plains (Badger back chasing the swallows, of course), Mrs Poser turned to Amble and said, "Well, after all that has happened today, I bet you're ready for your dinner!"

"*Oh,*" thought Amble, "*What a good idea.*"

As he gobbled down his food, he reflected on the day. It had been very scary getting stuck in the stream. But Mrs Poser had rescued him – she really was his favourite thing! And he had played out with Badger – his favourite thing. And come home and had his dinner. And now he had a very full tummy and was very tired.

Now it was time for bed – his favourite thing!

12.   A walk in the countryside

Mrs Poser folded away the map that she had been studying.

"Well, Amble," she said, "I know we had fun and games yesterday. But I am feeling so much better today. My nettle stings have disappeared completely. And I have discovered a new path on the map that we can explore. Would you like an adventure?"

Would Amble like an adventure? What do you think? Of course he would. Adventures are his favourite thing!

He wagged his tail and ran to the door.

But today wasn't as lovely and sunny as yesterday. The glorious hot autumn day of yesterday had come to an end, and now it was very clear that winter was coming. In fact, it was overcast and drizzling. There was also a penetrating sneaky wind that kept creeping up behind you and whistling through your fur.

So Mrs Poser dressed appropriately. She dug out her winter dog walking clothes and started to get ready. She put on her fleece and her waterproof jacket. Then she pulled on two pairs of socks – one pink pair, one blue pair. Then she put on her waterproof boots. Mrs Poser would not be cold today. And if Amble went into the stream with the steep sides again today, she would be much better prepared to save him, that was for sure. She wasn't going to make that mistake ever again.

Amble was getting very impatient. At last, Mrs Poser announced that she was ready.

Off they set.

They walked across the wild open plains.

As Amble ran along, he smelt something particularly enticing. Gosh, it was interesting. It smelt so good he just had to roll in it! Over and over again. It felt so good. He sniffed his tummy.

"*I smell delicious,*" he thought.

Mrs Poser didn't think so.

"Amble!" she shouted, in a VERY doom-laden voice – the one that she used only when Amble was in a LOT of trouble.

"Come here!"

She looked at Amble, and could smell what he had rolled in from quite some way away. It was disgusting.

Can you guess what Amble had been rolling in?

It was fox poo! It was incredibly smelly and horrible. Really disgusting!

Mrs Poser was so cross. They had walked a long way from the Big-House-On-The-Hill, and she didn't want to have to go back so that she could hose him down.

Then she had an idea.

Amble loved chasing sticks. It was his favourite thing. And Amble loved swimming. That was also his favourite thing. Mrs Poser knew this.

And, they could make a detour along the side of the stream which runs along the side of the wild open plains. It wouldn't add too many steps to the route…

Mrs Poser picked up three good dog-sized sticks. Just the

sort that Amble loved to chase. But she didn't show them to Amble. Not yet.

Mrs Poser walked well ahead of Amble, just in case they met anyone they knew (or even worse, someone they didn't know) and they tried to stroke Amble. Not that they would if the wind was behind them. They would smell him before they saw him! Yuck!

When they reached the banks of the stream where Mrs Poser was ABSOLUTELY sure Amble could get in AND out of the water, she shouted to Amble. Then, she threw one of the sticks into the water.

Well, Amble was beside himself with joy – a stick and a swim. And he had thought that he was in such trouble. Without another thought, he jumped straight into the stream and swam after the stick. Then he got out and brought it back to Mrs Poser, who threw it again – further into the stream this time so he had to swim further. Then she did it again with the next stick, and then the last stick!

When he brought the last stick back to Mrs Poser for the second time, she looked closely at him and sniffed the air around him.

"Good," she said with satisfaction. "That worked well!"

Amble didn't know what she meant until he realised that his lovely smell had disappeared. It had all been washed off by the stream. Well, that just wasn't fair. Mrs Poser had outsmarted him, and made him take off his lovely smell. And he hadn't even realised because he was having so much fun!

But he still had the rest of the walk to look forward to.

The intrepid pair continued along the cycle path until they reached a gate.

And who was waiting there but Badger and Mrs Pullalong. What a lovely surprise! Amble was beside himself with joy. Badger was very pleased to see Amble too. But it was a bit of a mystery why they were meeting here.

"It's lovely to see you!" woofed Badger. "But this isn't our usual place. Do you know what's going on?"

"Not a clue!" replied Amble, who really didn't care either. He was just so pleased to see his friend.

After all, Badger was his favourite thing.

Mrs Pullalong looked at Mrs Poser and asked "Do you know where we are supposed to be going next?"

In reply, Mrs Poser got out the map, and the ladies both looked at it with great interest.

Both the dogs started to get just the tiniest bit bored.

"The map says that we can turn right here, and walk along a bridle path. A bridle path is really for horses – so we had better watch out," said Mrs Poser.

Really, though, it wasn't necessary – the path was very overgrown, and you could hardly see it through all the long grass and thistles.

It was clear that since the cycle path had been built, people had stopped using this way as much. Amble could understand why. Those dratted thistles were at just the right height to hit him in the face as he ran on ahead.

However, now that people weren't using the path, Amble smelt that other animals were passing through. Indeed, he could smell the faintest aroma of foxes, and sighed. Before his swim, he had smelt so much better!

Badger was also not enjoying this walk as much as the one yesterday. The grass was too long and she couldn't find any swallows to play with. But she did agree with Amble that the hint of fox was quite enticing.

After what felt like hours walking through the rugged terrain, Amble spied another gate ahead of him.

"That gate is exactly where the map said it should be" explained Mrs Poser. "We go through there, across another field and then we will re-join the cycle path and walk home again."

The brave group went through the gate and started to cross the field. It smelt a lot like Amble had just a short time ago.

"There are no cows in this field, so the farmer must be fertilising the grass," said Mrs Poser as she held her nose with one hand and Amble's lead with the other. At least that's what Amble thought she said. It was difficult to hear because she had her hand over her nose!

But then, as they walked on, the source of the smell became obvious. The farmer had put a huge pile of cow dung directly in front of the next gate. Both the ladies were quite shocked. Mrs Pullalong decided that it was possibly the largest heap of manure that she had ever seen. It was almost the size of a small cottage! Mrs Poser thought it smelt horrid.

Amble quite liked it. In fact, he wondered if there was any way he could sneak away and roll in some of it before Mrs Poser would notice. Badger, quite wisely, said nothing, and kept well out of the way!

Mrs Poser came closer to the pile and discovered something terrible. She realised that not only did the pile smell disgusting, but the grass all around it, INCLUDING the path to the gate, was a mire of evil-looking brown liquid which stank just as much. And there was no choice. They had to go through this quagmire to get to the gate. There was simply no other way to go.

"Well," said Mrs Poser, "I suppose we have to bite the bullet and try to get across. It looks to be quite narrow here. I think I can jump across!"

With that, Mrs Poser put her best foot forward. And it sank. Right into the smelly mud. It went in so deep that the evil-looking brown liquid was almost level with the top of her boot. She tried to lift her foot up. It just wouldn't move. Even worse, she then had to put her other foot into the mess too, just to stay upright. Now Mrs Poser was in real trouble.

Amble watched from the edge and wondered what on earth she was doing.

Mrs Poser tried to jump. But her boots just wouldn't move. She couldn't keep her balance either, and started to wobble. And then she fell forwards and face down into the evil smelling mess.

Mrs Poser was covered in the gloopy dung from head to toe.

For a shocked second, no-one knew quite what to do next. But then, showing what she felt to be great presence of mind, Badger jumped onto Mrs Poser's back, and walked right across her to get to the gate!

Mrs Poser was speechless! Which was probably a good thing as she was still face down in the smelly mud.

Mrs Pullalong said, "Well, you are in a predicament! But it could solve our problem!"

"How do you work that one out?" slurped Mrs Poser, as she tried to stop any of the smelly brown liquid from going in her mouth.

"Well," continued Mrs Pullalong, as she hopped onto Mrs Poser's back as well, "You can't possibly get any dirtier, and if I walk across you, I won't get dirty at all!".

Which was true. But now Mrs Poser didn't know what to do. So she did what seemed best, which was nothing. She just lay very still as Mrs Pullalong, and then Amble, used her as a human bridge.

But she was such a sight when she got up. She was dripping from top to toe in cow poo. It was brown, smelly and everywhere! Even the tip of her nose.

Amble looked at her in absolute amazement and adoration. This woman was just fantastic. She rolled in cow poo – which he had to admit was a very good replacement for fox poo, and even let the lovely liquid go all over her. And even better, she had let him walk over her so he wouldn't get his feet wet. Given the cold wind, that was a very good thing. Amble was so proud of Mrs Poser!

Even Badger was impressed with just how delightfully smelly Mrs Poser was. Mrs Pullalong couldn't quite believe how disgustingly muddy Mrs Poser was.

But Amble was just a little bit jealous too. He had smelt better than that with the fox poo, and she had made him wash it off. Sometimes life was very unfair.

As for Mrs Poser, she was so embarrassed and she didn't know what to do next. The only way back was on the cycle path – and she was so muddy and smelly. What if she met someone she knew? Oh dear, oh dear! But they had no choice.

She stood up, and shook herself. And wrinkled her nose in disgust.

Then she started to walk. Amble thought that she was walking in a most peculiar way – then he realised that the evil mud had not only coated Mrs Poser's front, and all of her legs, but it was almost up to her waist. The wind made the gloopy mud feel even colder and slimier all the way up – and down – her legs. It clearly felt very, very unpleasant.

But once Mrs Poser had got used to feeling the effects of the sneaky, cold wind on her soaking, smelly clothes, she started to walk back very briskly, hoping no-one that she knew would see her.

Mrs Pullalong tried hard not to laugh. Poor Mrs Poser was indeed a bit of a mess.

"Why don't I go on ahead?" she said. "That way I can send Badger to warn you if I see anyone coming. Then you can hide in a hedge so they won't see you!"

Mrs Poser wasn't keen on this idea, but when she thought about it, it really was the only option. So she and Amble kept a safe distance behind.

They managed to walk a good distance without incident. Then, just as they reached the wild open plains: TROUBLE!

Badger came bouncing up to Mrs Poser, and she wasn't alone. Magic, the one blue-eye one brown-eye Border Collie was with her! That meant Gentleman Jim would not be far behind.

"Wow!" said Magic to Amble as he looked in admiration at Mrs Poser. "You must be so proud! Mrs Poser looks and smells just fab! I could smell her from right across the wild open plain!"

"I know!" said Amble, "But for some reason, she doesn't seem to like it!"

Meanwhile, Mrs Pullalong started to talk to Gentleman Jim and Mrs Poser tried to hide in the hedge. She wasn't very

successful. All that happened was her hair got very tangled in the hawthorns.

"What on earth have you two been up to now?" gasped Gentleman Jim, as he spied Mrs Poser covered in mud and leaves.

"It's a long story!" began Mrs Poser, "but could I ask you a favour?"

Can you guess what the favour was? Amble and Badger couldn't. Neither could Magic.

They all walked – very quickly – back to the Big-House-On-The-Hill. They arrived at the garden gate much sooner than they would have usually done as Mrs Poser was walking very briskly indeed.

Mrs Pullalong took the three dogs to play ball in the back garden. Amble was a little surprised – his walks usually ended with a rub down. Not his two friends coming to play.

Then things got even odder. Gentleman Jim strode over to the garden hosepipe. Then he switched it on. Amble was ready to hide. He hated the garden hose at any time, and it would be really unfair to wash him today! Not in front of his friends. He wasn't the one who smelt. Not today. And he wasn't dirty.

Clearly Gentleman Jim agreed. He pointed the hosepipe at Mrs Poser who stood under it and turned round and round. It took a long, long, time to wash the horrible smell off. Mrs Poser was quite, quite cold when they decided that she was finally clean enough to go into the Big-House-On-The-Hill without making too much mess.

"Why don't you go and have a proper shower and put those smelly things in the wash?" volunteered Mrs Pullalong. "I know where the tea things are. I'll make us a nice cup of tea, you clean up, and all will be right!"

Mrs Poser agreed. Clean skin, clean clothes and a cup of tea were definitely her favourite things!

13.   A perfect day

The phone rang. Amble woke up with a start. Why did that always happen? Just as he got to the really exciting bit in his dream (his favourite thing) where he had cornered the lion and was about to terrify it with his scary bark… Phones really were the most intrusive, noisy and annoying things.

Amble wished that Mrs Poser felt the same way. But no, she would chatter away for hours on it. And even worse, she had a spare one in her pocket for when they went out. He wished he had a dog biscuit for every time that one rang while they were walking.

No matter. He was awake now. He thought he had better go and find out what on earth had been so important. Amble shook himself, took one last sad look at his bed, and ran downstairs.

Mrs Poser looked excited. She patted Amble on the head (which was always a good sign, he felt. And, of course, one of his favourite things).

"We're going out this afternoon, Amble! And you will never guess where!"

Amble was all ears. And not his deaf ears either.

"Do you remember Adele?"

Of course he did. How could he forget Adele – she was his long lost sister – not that Mrs Poser knew that.

Amble also remembered why he hadn't seen her for such a long time. She was going to have puppies that would be Guide Dogs when they grew up.

"This afternoon, we are going to see her. And her puppies!"

"I'm an uncle!" thought Amble, and rushed off to tell Teaser and Wafter.

"Amble – come back here!" shouted Mrs Poser "There is more to tell you!"

But it was too late – Amble had rushed into the back garden and was barking at the potting shed door!

"Wake up, Wafter!" he yelped. "Come here, Teaser, please…"

Both Wafter and Teaser were in the middle of a local mouse hunt. The unfortunate rodent had accidentally wandered into the potting shed, and now they had it cornered.

"Drat!" muttered Wafter, as the barking broke their concentration. The mouse took advantage and darted past Wafter and, despite Teaser's best efforts, squeezed past them both and ran through the cat flap to freedom.

"Please come here," continued Amble, barking away and totally oblivious to the situation.

"This had better be good," snarled Wafter, as she was very unhappy at losing the mouse. She had invested quite some time in rounding it up. Teaser was also not best pleased as he had played a big supporting role in cornering the little blighter, and was just as cross that it had managed to escape.

Both cats stalked out through the cat flap and stood disdainfully in front of Amble.

Wafter looked at Amble using her absolute disgust expression, the one that she used when things were just beyond the pale.

"And, what, pray tell me," she asked in a scornful voice, "is so important that we have to break off from rodent duty, AND before milk break, in the middle of an important interrogation, to listen to you?"

Amble was jumping about the place like a mad thing. Like he was chasing a ball, only there wasn't one.

"I'm an uncle!" he shouted. "I'm an uncle!"

"Is that it?" asked Teaser, amazed that Amble had disturbed their morning's work for this.

"Harrumph!" said Wafter. She couldn't trust herself to say anything else. After all, she wanted to continue to live here. The dog might be here, but the food was still good and Mrs Poser did so enjoy her company. If Wafter said what she really thought, Mrs Poser might ask her to leave!

But Amble was too excited to even begin to realise that the cats couldn't care less. He was so happy. He now had a sister, and nieces and nephews. Or maybe it was nephews and nieces. Or just nephews? Or nieces? Amble thought it might be sensible to go back to Mrs Poser and see if he could find out.

Amble ran back to the house and to the bottom of the stairs, where Mrs Poser was still standing.

"I'm glad you've decided to come back!" she sniffed. "I have more to tell you. But if you're not interested – and you clearly aren't or you wouldn't have run off like that – I won't bother!"

Amble looked pleadingly upward, with his eyes on full amber.

"Oh, please, please – tell me as much as you can. I need to know! I'm sorry I ran off like that, but I had to tell Teaser and Wafter about the puppies!"

Of course, Mrs Poser didn't understand any of this – she doesn't speak Dog. All she could hear was Amble whimpering.

"Oh Amble!" she said, in that forgiving tone that he knew too well.

Then, she went on to tell him more about the telephone call.

Adele had had six puppies – three little boys and three little girls. And apparently Mr Helpful had said that she and Amble could go and visit them today!

"That's if you want to?" she asked.

Did he want to? Well, what do you think? The afternoon just couldn't come quickly enough.

Eventually, though, it was time to go

Mrs Poser got the car out and told Amble to get in.

"It's a bit of a walk to Mr Helpful's house, so we'll drive."

Amble thought that was a jolly good idea. He loved travelling in cars. They were his favourite thing!

So in he leapt, and settled down while Mrs Poser put his seat belt on. Then she put her seat belt on, started the car, and off they went.

It wasn't that far to Mr Helpful's house, but it seemed to take ages to Amble. He couldn't get there quickly enough. Which is completely the opposite of how Amble usually felt about travelling in the car. Usually, he wanted the journey to take forever and ever. But he had so missed his sister since that lovely day on the wild open plains.

Amble barked loudly as the car pulled into the drive. Mr Helpful came to the door and opened it with a huge smile on his face.

"How lovely to see you both!" he said, as Amble struggled out of his seat belt.

"I should warn you – I am expecting a few more visitors today. Adele so wants to show off her brood, and so do I! I've made tea and cake for everyone too!"

Amble decided that he liked Mr Helpful even more. Tea and cake were his favourite things.

As they walked through the door, Mrs Poser muttered in Amble's ear – "Please behave yourself, Amble. And don't steal any cake!"

Amble could hear the noise of youngsters playing, and in the background, he could make out Adele's gentle voice saying, "Don't do that to your sister, Jack," and, "Jill, stop biting your brother's ear, you know he doesn't like it!"

Gosh. They were here. Really here. Amble couldn't wait to see Adele, and to meet his new family. But he also knew that he had to be on his best behaviour or he might not get to see them after all – so near and yet so far.

Mr Helpful led the way into the brightly decorated kitchen where Adele and the puppies were.

Amble just stared. He couldn't believe his eyes. There were more puppies than his paws could count! Mrs Poser looked surprised too. And in the middle of it all, looking totally relaxed and calm, was Adele. She looked so well and happy.

Each puppy had a name beginning with "J" – although Mrs Poser privately thought that calling them "One" to "Six" might have been more sensible. And how on earth could you tell them apart?

"Here they are!" he said. "There's Jack and Jill – they were born first; then there is Jumper and Juniper, and Janey and Jemma! Quite a handful, aren't they! But when they grow up, they will all become Guide Dogs if they work hard.

You could tell that he was so proud, of them and Adele.

Mr Helpful told them that he did have problems recognising which pup was which – so much so that he had had to put a blob of nail varnish on the paws of each one. A different colour for each pup, of course. Otherwise it wouldn't have worked.

Meanwhile, Amble was awestruck. He gazed at Adele. She smiled contentedly back at him.

"Hello," she said. "Children – meet your uncle."

All the puppies turned to look at Amble, and then all of them rushed to lick him.

Mrs Poser had never seen anything quite like this before at all. Not ever. And Mr Helpful was a bit surprised.

However, he thought he might have an explanation. And it was such a big surprise, that Mrs Poser was really shocked!

"I've been doing a bit of research on Adele, and who her family is," began Mr Helpful. "I wanted to know so that I could tell Guide Dog School. And do you know what I found out?"

Do you think you might know? Amble did, but Mrs Poser didn't.

"Adele is Amble's big sister!" announced Mr Helpful. "Look – I have all the paperwork to prove it!"

Oh my goodness me! Mrs Poser had to sit down. She looked through the letters that Mr Helpful gave to her, and agreed. Yes – Amble was indeed Adele's brother.

"How amazing!" she said. "Isn't it a small world! I suppose I should have guessed when I watched them playing."

Amble, meanwhile, was totally oblivious to all that was going on. He was having such a wonderful time letting the puppies climb all over him as Adele watched on.

As Mrs Poser was starting to compose herself, there was a knock at the door. This must be the other visitors that Mr Helpful had mentioned.

Mr Helpful went to the door, and as he talked to the person, another Golden Labrador walked into the kitchen. It was clear that this Labrador was very old, and she was very stiff. She was very proper. But she walked briskly up to Adele nevertheless.

"Hello, Mother," said Adele. "Or should I call you Grandma?"

Amble's ears pricked up over the noise of the children.

"Mother? Grandma?" he thought. *"It couldn't be. Could it? Might it be? Oh gosh! What if it was? What would happen?"*

Mr Helpful and Mrs Poser watched what happened next from the door.

Adele smiled on.

"Children. Leave your uncle alone for a minute. This is your grandma. She's travelled a long, long way to see you, so make a huge fuss of her!"

As the puppies ran towards the elderly Labrador, Adele spoke to her mother.

"Mummy," she said, "I have another surprise for you. Look who else is here!"

Amble sniffed his way across, following in the wake of the youngsters. He was as close to the floor as you could get because he was frightened that Mummy might not want to see him. Or that she would still be very cross about what happened at Guide Dog School. Or both....

But Mother looked at Amble, and then gave him the biggest lick ever and said:

"Amble. Oh, Amble – I thought I would never see you ever again. I've missed you so much. You were the naughtiest of any of my children, but you could always make me laugh. I've missed you so much!"

Mrs Poser was almost crying, watching the three dogs. Mr Helpful sneezed into a hankie.

The puppies decided to climb back onto Amble. All of them thought he was just the best bouncy castle ever (and Mrs Poser

made a mental note to get Amble back on his diet when they got back home. No more treats for you, my boy!)

As Mrs Poser, Mr Helpful and the other visitors helped themselves to tea and cake, Adele and Amble snuggled up to Mother. The puppies all gathered round. They wanted to hear Adele tell some stories about their uncle and how he used to nibble her ear when she was little. Amble decided that he wanted to listen too. Grandma Labrador decided that she would have a snooze.

Life was just perfect, thought Amble. Just how it should be.

He wanted to run up to Mrs Poser and to Mr Helpful and give them both lots and lots of licks to say thank you for making this afternoon happen. He also wanted to cuddle his Mother close and never let her go. But he also remembered that Adele was the best storyteller ever, and he wanted to listen to her.

Sometimes, the best thing to do is nothing, and just let things happen. So that's exactly what Amble did.

And it was perfect.

A really perfect day.

And just his favourite thing.

14. Dreams

It's evening time at the Big-House-On-The-Hill, and all is quiet. Amble is tucked up in his bed. Mrs Poser sits downstairs, drinking her bedtime cup of tea and eating her last ginger biscuit of the day before heading upstairs.

As she sips the tea, Mrs Poser is thinking about how Amble has changed her life. Not always in the way she might have expected, but things have certainly not been dull since he arrived.

She remembers that very first Christmas when Amble arrived. He was so frightened and scared, but so excited too. She smiles as she remembers how he jumped and romped across the garden, and his surprise and delight when he discovered the pond.

Thankfully, things seem to have settled down quite a lot since then, although the two of them have managed to find themselves in a lot of mischief and scrapes.

Mrs Poser reflects that until Amble arrived, she had never been stuck in a stream, stung by nettles or taken her tee shirt off anywhere other than her bedroom. And she would never have worn it inside out anywhere!

As for being covered in cow poo, and having to be hosed down – well that was just beyond anything she could have imagined…

But, as she takes another bite of the ginger biscuit, Mrs Poser muses that without Amble, she would never have met Mrs Pullalong, Mr Helpful or Gentleman Jim. They are such good friends now, and she can't really remember what it was like before she met them.

Indeed, an awful lot had happened since Amble arrived, and although he can be just the naughtiest dog, he is loving and kind. And he really doesn't mean to be naughty. Although she would only ever admit it to herself – she loves him to bits.

Back in the potting shed, the cats are gearing up for their early evening patrol of the perimeter. They are so glad that Amble is asleep. They can get on without being interrupted and do their jobs properly. There seem to be more mice and rats than ever these days, and it's so important that they don't come anywhere near to the Big-House-On-The-Hill.

In another house, not too far away, That Baby is also asleep. She is dreaming of her next visit to the Big-House-On-The-Hill, and of playing with Amble. She smiles in her sleep as she thinks of throwing food at him, and watching him gobble it up. And of chasing the cats, and chewing their tails! Definitely her favourite things!

Amble snoozes on, oblivious to what the rest of the world is doing. He is dreaming of his life and how he loves being here at the Big-House-On-The-Hill. It's his favourite thing, you know!

Just like every other night when he finally goes to bed, he is quite worn out. So much so that he snores away on his bed almost before his head hits the blanket. But even so, he still has time to dream. Amble dreams a lot. Every so often, he yelps and twitches in his sleep as he recalls everything that has happened! Like Amble himself, his dreams are messy, full of action and fun.

And in his dreams, Mrs Poser is always there. But she never tells him off in his dreams – no matter what mischief he gets up to. Not like in real life. He hates being told off, especially by Mrs Poser's Voice of Doom, which is no surprise.

As Amble snoozes on, he remembers back to his first few weeks of settling in. Gosh, it was hard to make friends with the cats. He liked them, but they were so suspicious of him. Even now, he doesn't really think they are his friends, but at least they talk to him. They don't run away and hide when he comes into the room any

more. But he has had to accept that he certainly isn't their favourite thing!

And really, it doesn't matter that much to Amble whether the cats want him to be their friend or not any more. He's made lots of other lovely friends since he moved in with Mrs Poser. Now, as he sleeps on, he dreams of playing with them. He loves his friends Badger and Magic to bits. They are such fun! In fact, they are his favourite thing!

He remembers the first time Badger and Magic came to the Big-House-On-The-Hill and how they chased Teaser upstairs into Mrs Poser's bedroom. Gosh, they were all so naughty that day! Maybe that's why the cats don't want to be friends?

Then there was the time he followed Badger into the steep-sided stream. Amble remembers how he got stuck in the stream, and how Mrs Poser bravely clambered in to rescue him, then she got stuck herself. Amble chuckles to himself as he remembered how funny Mrs Poser looked with her tee shirt with the red label on inside out! That memory is possibly his favourite thing!

Amble sighs heavily as he remembers the expression on Mrs Poser's face as she fell into the cow poo. She wasn't at all happy! But she did smell divine. Amble is still puzzled why it wasn't one of Mrs Poser's favourite things.

Dreams of cow poo merge with getting lost in Mystery Woods. Amble yelps and barks in his sleep because that was so scary... Then, he calms down as he dreams about chasing the swallows with Badger, and the ball with Magic. You know, swallows and balls are pretty high on his list of favourite things!

He dreams of winter, of cold weather, and having to wait for Mrs Poser to get ready for walks. Gosh, she takes forever!

Then images of That Baby and Christmas come to mind. Oh, how he loved Christmas with That Baby. All that food, the paper mess and more food! Amble really loves the way that That Baby throws food on the floor, and leaves biscuits on the chairs. She really should visit more often. Yes, Christmas and That Baby are definitely his favourite things.

As he snuggles closer to the radiator, he starts to get warm, and in his dream, he remembers summer. His trip to the seaside, the sound of the sea, and its salty taste. He remembers how the shops all seem brighter and more colourful than the ones in town. And that there was an almost limitless supply of gritty ice cream on the ground. He licks his lips in his sleep as he remembers all the ice cream that he found on the ground. Oh yes, most definitely a favourite thing!

Then he thinks of cheddar cheese sandwiches and that strange game that humans play. What was it called? Oh yes, that's right – cricket! But if he had to choose, it would be the cheddar cheese sandwiches, and not the cricket, which is his favourite thing! Much tastier.

Then, he dreams about his family. His real family....

A slow smile works its way across his face when he thinks of Adele. It has made him so happy to find his sister again. He really loves his sister, and he is so proud of her. Fancy her not being a Guide Dog! And fancy her having puppies! He loves being an uncle – it could possibly be his favourite thing! It was just lovely how his nieces and nephews all climbed all over him and said that he was their favourite thing.

He is beside himself with happiness that he has seen his mother again, after all this time. He whimpers with sheer joy that she still loves him and isn't cross with him about what happened at Guide Dog School. He missed her so much.

And now he has three nieces and three nephews to love as well. But being reunited with Mummy, that is definitely his favourite thing.

Across the wild open plains, in Mrs Pullalong's home, Badger is gently napping between walks. It will soon be time for her late night stroll (that's the one where she actually walks rather than sprints). She hopes it will be on the wild open plains where she may see the cats. Not that they talk to each other when they do see each other. Not even to say hello. And there won't be any swallows to chase as they will all be snug in their nests at this late hour, but she might spot a lost fox or rabbit to chase.

Badger hopes that she will see Amble again tomorrow, and wonders what future adventures they might have.

I am thinking the same. Aren't you?

It's my favourite thing.